Eighty-Eight Steps
to September

Eighty-Eight Steps to September

JAN MARINO

Little, Brown and Company
Boston   Toronto   London

First edition

Library of Congress Cataloging-in-Publication Data
Marino, Jan. Eighty-eight steps to September : a novel /
by Jan Marino. — 1st ed.
p.   cm.
Summary: A little girl's happy life changes when she
learns her brother isn't going to come home from the
hospital.
ISBN 0-316-54620-8
[1. Death — Fiction.   2. Brothers and sisters — Fiction.]   I. Title.   PZ7.M33884Ei   1989   [Fic] —
dc19   88-39873   CIP   AC

10 9 8 7 6 5 4 3 2 1

Published simultaneously in Canada
by Little, Brown & Company (Canada) Limited
Printed in the United States of America

Eighty-Eight Steps to September

Prologue

If I were to find an eyelash on my cheek, and if I were to place it on my finger, make a wish, and blow it away, I know where my wish would take me. I would be standing at the very top of the 88's, just before dark. Sam would be running circles around me, barking, wanting to get on home. But I'd tell him to be still.

"I'm waiting for someone," I'd say. And then I'd sit and pull Sam close to me, and the two of us would look down to the bottom of the 88's to where all of Manuet stretched out before our eyes.

"Look, Sam," I'd say. "There's Miss Buxton closing up the bakeshop. And there's Miss Finnegan running to catch the last trolley. Just like always."

Way across town, we'd see the harbor and maybe we'd get to see an old tugboat chug on by. And then we'd look clear across the harbor to Boston, where one by one the lights would begin to come on. We'd watch until the sky above the harbor was dotted with little patches of light.

"Amy," I'd hear a voice call in the distance. "Hey, Amy, you going to sit there all night?"

And there he'd be, standing at the bottom of the

88's. Same as always. His hair would be bleached from the sun. His face would be tanned and his arms and legs would be strong again.

"It's him," I'd yell in Sam's ear. "It's Robbie."

I'd jump up and run down the stairs to where he stood, and when I got there, Sam would leap out of my arms and into his. Sam would bark and lick his face and his ears, and Robbie would laugh the way he used to.

"Hey, Amy," he'd say after a while, "race you up." And before I could answer, he'd be flying up, Sam in his arms, me trailing behind him, but just before he got to the top, he'd stop and wait so the two of us could walk up together. And when we got to the very top, I'd put my arms around his neck and never let him go. Never. Ever. If I had an eyelash to wish on.

1

"I don't like it any better than you do, Robbie," my mother said. "But Baron has got to go to the farm. We can't keep him cooped up. He's miserable in Manuet."

The door to Robbie's room slammed shut. "Robbie," I heard her say, "Dad's leaving for Uncle Sam's in about an hour. Please don't make it harder for everybody than it already is."

Robbie didn't answer, and after a little while, my mother walked down the hall and back into her bedroom.

I sat on the edge of my bed and looked around my room. It wouldn't be the same without Baron. He didn't mean to scare people. He just wanted to be friends. But the mailman told my mother he wouldn't deliver the mail anymore. And the milkman told her she'd have to go to the grocery store to buy milk, because every time he pulled his truck into the driveway, Baron would jump inside and it would take two of us to get him out.

The last time my mother and father went to Boston and Mrs. Breene came to spend the night with us, I tried to convince her to take Baron home with her.

"Amy, I'd love to," she'd said, "but I can't. Mr. Breene wouldn't hear of it. Why, Baron must eat close to thirty pounds of dog food a week."

Poor Baron. He was such a sweet dog. He couldn't help it if he was only two years old and weighed a hundred and fifty pounds.

"He's too big to live in a place like Manuet," my mother kept telling us. "It's like keeping an elephant in a trailer. It's not fair to him."

Sometimes I hate living in Manuet. Everybody knows everybody else's business. "Morning, Amy, how you doing in school this year?" Miss Buxton calls from the bakeshop. I swear she can see from the side of her head, because no matter how fast I fly by that store, she calls out, "Morning, Amy."

Then there're the stairs. Everybody calls them the 88's, but I counted them once, and there are only eighty-three. I can't go to school or to the beach or anywhere without having to climb those stairs. My father says I should be glad to live in a town with such history. "Before the town built the stairs," he always says, "the British slid down the hill and lost a major battle."

I guess the stairs are okay, but sometimes they're a pain, like when you're in a real hurry.

But the worst thing about Manuet is Miss Swords. She's the old crab who lives on our corner and who's always complaining about Baron. Every time I come near her house, she jumps out of her rocking chair, picks up that stupid cat of hers, and calls out, "Amory Martin, you get that big, old animal off my side-

7

walk . . ." Then she goes back to her rocker and says, "Now, now, Sweet Sally, don't get upset. You just calm down now, dearie."

My brother, Robbie, is thirteen and he tells me to ignore her, but sometimes I can't. One day I called her cat a name and she called my mother, who made me go back and apologize.

"I have to apologize to the cat?"

"You have to apologize to Miss Swords, or you'll spend Saturday up in your room."

There was no choice. I apologized to the cat.

Driving up to the farm, everybody was very quiet. My father didn't even put on his Frank Sinatra station. My sister, Susan, who is fifteen and thinks she is the most sophisticated person in the entire state of Massachusetts, sat in the front seat. Robbie was in the back of the wagon with Baron, and I was alone in the middle seat. Every once in a while, I'd turn and pet Baron. Even he was quiet.

My mother hadn't come. I knew she felt bad about sending Baron to live on the farm. "It's like sending an old person to a rest home," she'd said to my father when she thought I wasn't listening.

I listen all the time. Every chance I get, I listen. My mother says only sneaks do that, but I don't think that is necessarily so. I don't think I'm a sneak. I just like to know what's going on, and when you're eleven, you don't find out anything unless you listen. And so that's what I do.

Just before we got to the farm, my father slowed

down the car and said, "I know it's hard for all of you to leave Baron, especially you, Rob . . ."

Boy, did that get me mad. Everyone always said that to Robbie, like Baron belonged to him. "Baron belongs to every — "I started to say, but my father went right on talking.

". . . but Uncle Sam is really fond of Baron. He'll have a good home and we'll visit, so it isn't as though you're saying good-bye forever. And Aunt Emma will be good for him, too. She's got a big heart for animals and people. She was awfully good to me when my mother died."

It made me sad to think my father was only a little boy when his mother died. I put my elbows on the top of the front seat and leaned my head on his shoulder. He reached back and pulled my pigtail.

"Rob, did you hear me?" he said. "We'll be there in a few minutes."

But Robbie didn't answer.

When we turned onto the road leading to the farm, I saw my Aunt Emma sitting on the porch glider. My father tooted the horn, and she waved her arms over her head and started down the porch steps.

"Where's Sam?" my father called to her. Then he got out of the car and picked her up, hugged her hard, and swung her around.

He always did that and Aunt Emma loved it. She'd pretend she didn't, and she'd always say stuff like "Oh, aren't you the one," or "You put me right down," but her face said something else.

"Oh, aren't you something," Aunt Emma said,

smoothing her hair and then her dress. "Sam's out back in the barn. Go down and fetch him. He's been waiting for you all morning." Then she looked over at us and said, "Come on out of that hot car. I'll fix us some cool lemonade."

Susan got out and gave her a kiss. Aunt Emma kissed her back about a hundred times and then called out, "Come on, you two. I've got fresh gingerbread in the oven."

But Robbie didn't move. He stayed in the back of the wagon, his arm around Baron. I started to open the door but he climbed over the seat and pulled my arm back. Then he rolled up all the windows and locked the doors.

"What're you doing?" I said.

"Baron's not staying here," he said. "I'm not opening this car until Dad says he comes home." Then he looked straight at me, his lips barely moving, and said, "Either you get out now, or you stay until Baron gets to come home. You hear me?"

"Sure," I said, "I hear you. I'll stay. I'll stay forever."

Aunt Emma motioned for us to get out of the car, but Rob shook his head and shouted, "No."

I leaned back, rubbed Baron's neck, and shook my head. "No," I said, putting my face into Baron's thick, soft fur. "No."

Aunt Emma came closer and Baron began to bark. He pulled away from me and leaped into the driver's seat. He sat there and barked so loud I couldn't hear what Aunt Emma was saying, but she looked upset. Susan ran over and put her face near the windshield.

Baron licked at her through the window, and even though he began to bark louder, I knew what she was saying: "What do you two think you're doing? Open the door."

But we didn't, and Robbie kept saying, "You're coming home, boy. You're coming home."

Aunt Emma turned away from us and started to walk real fast toward the barn.

"Shhh. Shhh," I said, putting my arm around Baron. "Be quiet. You'll see. We'll get you home." But Baron didn't quiet down, and from the back window, I could see my father coming up from the barn. His hair was blowing around and he looked angry. Uncle Sam was holding Taffy, Aunt Emma's cat, and trying to keep up with my father. I could see his bushy white eyebrows moving up and down, and he was shaking his head back and forth. He stopped for a minute, took off his cap, and wiped his face on his sleeve. Then he turned and handed Taffy to my aunt.

It was so hot in the car I could hardly breathe, and my stomach felt funny. I opened the front window just a little. Baron kept jumping from one window to another, barking like crazy, and when he saw Taffy, he began to howl. My father walked over to the car. His face was red, and when he came near the window, I could hear him say, "Open the door, Rob. You're making it difficult for all of us."

But Robbie didn't move. Neither did I.

I got Baron to stop barking, but he was so hot he started to pant and then he drooled all over the seats. "Robbie," my father said, "please open the door."

"I'm not opening the door until you say Baron can come home." Robbie looked like he was going to cry. "Please, Dad. Please."

My father reached into his pocket, took out the keys, and tried to open the front door, but Robbie held the lock down. My father's ears looked like sliced beets. Then he looked right at me, and said, "Amy. Open the door. Now."

"Don't do it. They'll take Baron for sure," Robbie said.

I looked back at my father, bit my lip, and said, "I won't, Rob."

This was the first time in my whole life I didn't do what my father asked me to do. It felt scary. He shook his head and then walked around to the back of the wagon and tried to open the door, but the safety lock was down.

Uncle Sam came over and peered in the front window and said, "Hi there, Baron. We got your bed out on the back porch and Sari and Elmer are waitin' for you."

Baron was so excited he kept banging his head on the steering wheel trying to get at Uncle Sam. He began to howl louder, and then he began to pant real bad.

"Robbie," Uncle Sam said in a low voice, "you ain't doin' Baron a favor keepin' him in this hot machine. You ain't doin' him no good at all." Then he turned and said something to my father, and the two of them walked up to the front porch where Aunt Emma and Susan were.

Robbie sat back, trying to calm Baron down, but it was no use. Every time he saw Taffy, he'd begin to howl. Then he'd pace back and forth and kind of cry.

"You think he'll take a fit or something?" I said. "Bootsy's cat took a fit when she got stuck in the hamper."

Robbie didn't answer me. He just kept rubbing Baron's neck, nuzzling his face into his fur. Baron whimpered and licked Rob's face and the top of his head.

"He's miserable in here," Robbie said, "even with me."

I slid over and put my arm around Baron. "Remember the day he jumped the fence and took all the cereal samples the new mailman was delivering?"

Robbie nodded his head.

"Remember how he told Momma he was going to report her and Baron to the postmaster?"

Robbie laughed a little.

"Maybe Baron will like it here after a while," I said, not really believing it. Then I leaned back and didn't say anything. Robbie kept petting Baron's head. I just watched. I could see my father sitting on the porch with everybody. Waiting.

After a long time, Robbie said, "Do me a favor, will you, Ame?"

"Sure," I said. "Anything."

"Take Baron in and be sure to tell Aunt Emma how much he likes it when you put a little milk in his water."

"But maybe Daddy will change his mind."

"He won't." Then Robbie put his arms around Baron

and without saying anything, said good-bye. He pushed Baron and said, "Go on, Baron. You've got to go."

"He doesn't want to go," I said.

Robbie shrugged his shoulders.

I got out of the car and walked slowly to the porch. Baron pulled on his collar and looked back at the car, but Rob was turned toward the field.

"Rob," I called, "Baron doesn't want to."

But he wouldn't answer me. I stood there for a long minute and then let Baron's collar go. Just as I did, Taffy came out from underneath the porch, and Baron took off after her. Taffy ran back and hid under the steps until my aunt came and coaxed her into her arms.

"This here is Baron," Aunt Emma told Taffy, "and you're too old to carry on with the likes of him, so you might as well make up your mind to be friends." Then Aunt Emma put her hand on Baron's head and said, "That goes for you, too, old boy."

And without another word, Aunt Emma climbed up the porch steps with Taffy in her arms and Baron at her heels, his tail wagging so hard it banged the sides of the stair railing. I called to Baron, but he kept going. And when the screen door slammed shut behind them, I swallowed real hard, walked back to the car, and waited to go home.

2

I woke up real slow the next morning. Usually I'd jump out of bed and take Baron out to the backyard to let him run around for a while. But this morning was different. Baron wasn't here.

When we had gotten back from the farm, everybody was quiet. I hated that. My father went into his study and my mother went up to her room. Susan went over to Stanley's, and Robbie went out on the back porch. I sat in the kitchen by myself. I could hear the glider squeak, and then I heard it bang against the porch wall, and when Robbie let it go, I could feel it under my feet. It squeaked and banged for a long time. And when the glider stopped, I heard something else. I put my hand over my ears, but I could still hear it. So I hummed. First soft. Then loud. Then loud loud, until I couldn't hear Robbie crying anymore.

"Are you up?" my mother's voice called from the kitchen.

I stretched my arms, pushed the covers off with my feet, and slid out of bed. It was so bright it hurt my eyes to look outside. It was the last week of school, my favorite time of the year. Today, the books got collected and we got to vote for the kids who would march in the moving-up day exercises.

"Amy," my mother called again, "it's getting late. Robbie, come on. Sue, your breakfast is getting cold."

"I'll be down in a minute," I yelled.

I went to my closet and took out my plaid dress. I hated it, but my father liked it, so I decided to wear it. Last night he was kind of mad at me — not really mad mad, but kind of mad. "Amy," he'd said, "you didn't help any of us by going along with Robbie. Especially Rob."

I put on the stupid dress and pulled my socks on. I picked up a dirty sock from the floor, spit on it, and shined my shoes. Then I looked in the mirror. I looked terrible; the sleeves were tight and I couldn't find the belt. And the cowlick on the left side of my head made my bangs look like a squashed broom. I started toward the bathroom to wash up, hoping my mother wouldn't catch me dressed and not washed. She hated that. "I can never understand how you can dress without washing and brushing your teeth first," she'd always say. But I liked to do it that way. And besides, I was never that dirty.

When I walked by Robbie's room, I could see him lying on the floor looking up at his fish tank. He never got tired of watching them.

"You're going to be late for school, Rob."

He didn't turn around. He just shrugged his shoulders.

"It's so quiet here without Baron," I said. "Remember how he used to bang his tail against the tank and the fish would go all crazy? And remember the time he tried to catch one and knocked the tank over and the water leaked into the kitchen and Momma got so mad she made Baron sleep in the garage?"

Robbie nodded and started to laugh a little. It was good to hear him laugh. He got up and put some food in the tank and swished it around with his finger.

"Robbie, do you want to walk to school with Celie and me?"

"Are you crazy?" he said.

I poked my head in the door, and said, "How come it doesn't bother you when Gloreen Denney asks you to walk her home? Answer me that," I said.

"Because Gloreen isn't a pain like you and Celie."

"Well, for your information," I said, "Celie's singing teacher lives next door to Gloreen, and his son, Ralphie, told Celie that Gloreen still wets the bed. So there's your glamorous Gloreen."

Robbie turned and looked at me and then leaped over his bed.

I raced down the hall and into the bathroom and slammed the door behind me. I could hear him yelling I was a blabbermouth and if I ever told anybody that disgusting story about Gloreen, he'd break my arm.

He started to bang on the door. "Did you hear me, Amy?"

"Yes, Robert, I heard you. I heard you," I said, turning on the water.

"If you don't shut up about Gloreen, I'll tell every kid in your class you still sleep with your dolls."

That did it. I opened the door and stuck my head out. "You big squealer. Go ahead and tell them. And you know what I'll tell Momma? Remember the time you tied the sheet to your bed and sneaked out the window? Remember that? I'll tell her that."

Robbie shoved me back into the bathroom and said, "Just don't tell anybody what you said about Gloreen."

"I'll think about it," I said. Then I slammed the door shut and locked it.

He gave the door a couple of bangs and said, "Remember what I said."

I finished getting washed, and then I tried to get my bangs to stay down with some of my mother's hair stuff, but it was no use. They just looked like a wet squashed broom.

In the kitchen, my father was reading the paper and my mother was drinking her coffee. I knew my mother had fixed breakfast, because there was oatmeal with wheat germ and raisins. My mother sometimes works at the hospital as a dietitian and she doesn't believe in serving anything that tastes good. Lots of times my father cooks breakfast and even dinner. My mother isn't allowed to tell him what to cook, so the food tastes better.

My father put down his paper. I smiled and he smiled back.

"That's a nice dress," he said. "I've always liked plaid."

I smiled more. I hated anybody to be even a little mad at me. Especially my father. Maybe because he

hardly ever got mad at anybody. I finished my breakfast real fast, grabbed my books, and yelled good-bye.
I raced through my backyard, up the hill, across the
field, and down the convent hill to the top of the 88's.
Celie was waiting for me.

"Hey, Amy," she called. "Hurry up. We get to pick
the kids for the moving-up exercises today."

When I caught up to Celie, we flew down the stairs
and into the schoolyard and got to our room just as
the bell rang.

"Good morning, ladies and gentlemen," Miss Finnegan said.

Miss Finnegan was about the most hated teacher in
the school. She had hair that looked like black-and-
white Brillo. Her teeth were okay, except she always
got lipstick on them and they kind of clicked when she
talked. I wouldn't have minded that, or even her hair,
if she were nice. But she wasn't. She was always saying
things like the "ladies and gentlemen" thing and then
she wouldn't let anybody laugh when she said it. But
this morning some of the kids started to laugh.

"Yes," she said, "I said ladies and gentlemen. That's
exactly what you'll be expected to be when you move
upstairs to Miss Alexander's sixth grade come September. I am sure, as sure as my name is Miss Margaret
Finnegan and this day is the twenty-third day of June
in the year 1948, she will not take the nonsense I have
taken."

I tried to think of the nonsense Miss Finnegan took.
We were all so scared of her that once I bit my lip to

stop laughing and it started to bleed. I wanted my mother to switch me into Miss Botwinik's class, but she wouldn't. "You have to deal with all types of people, Amy," she'd said. "That's part of growing up." And so I got stuck with Miss Finnegan.

Miss Finnegan began to walk toward the back row. I turned and saw Bootsy Russell smiling. "You find that amusing, Mr. Russell?" she said. Some of the kids started to laugh because it sounded so funny to hear Bootsy be called Mr. Russell. Bootsy never combed his hair and he always picked his nose. After Celie, Bootsy was my best friend, but I never let him put his right hand on anything of mine. That was the hand he picked his nose with.

Miss Finnegan whirled around and shouted, "That's enough. I'm leaving school at the noon recess, so if you want to select the people for the various honor positions for the moving-up exercises, you'd better settle down. Now."

She looked at us over her glasses and said, "There are five honor positions. You are to select one person in each category. Peter, would you give each person a slip of paper, which you'll find on top of my desk?"

Roberta Barry raised her hand and said, "Miss Finnegan, are we going to vote for just anybody, or are you going to put names on the board?"

It was just like Roberta to ask that. Everybody hated her, except Miss Finnegan and Peter Morgan. Roberta and Peter were Miss Finnegan's favorites. They got to pass out the milk, and Roberta sold cookies at recess.

She even got to be yard monitor. She wore a special belt and she reported all the kids to Miss Finnegan. She was a pain.

"Roberta, my dear," Miss Finnegan said, "much as I'd like to nominate certain people for these places of honor, Mr. Mueller feels that since this is the class's moving-up day, the class should vote for whomever they wish."

Celie looked over at me and smiled. We both knew if Miss Finnegan picked the kids out, Peter would sing the school anthem and carry the flag. Carol and Cathy Schultz would carry the banner, because they matched. Roberta would lead the kids into the auditorium and carry a baton on her shoulder, and Celie and I would be at the end of the pageant with Bootsy.

When the class finished voting, Miss Finnegan counted the votes and said, "Cecelia DiCarlo has been selected to carry the flag and sing the school anthem. There is a tie for the honor guard — Amory Martin and Marilyn Rabe. Theodore Russell and Timothy Gavin will carry the banner. Patrick Youngs, as class representative, will lead the salute to the flag and give his speech." Then, peering over her glasses, she said, "You are to dress in appropriate attire. Absolutely no sneakers."

I couldn't believe it. Celie got to sing and carry the flag; Marilyn and I got to lead the kids into the auditorium; and Bootsy got to carry half the banner. Some of the kids started to clap, and a couple of kids started to jump around.

"Settle down," Miss Finnegan shouted. "Settle

down." And then she asked us to take out our reading books until it was time for the noon recess. "There will be a short test on the last two chapters before the noon bell rings."

When the bell finally rang, everybody leaped out of their seats. Celie and I ate our lunch, then bought our cookies and ran out into the schoolyard. We went over to where the kids were playing jump rope and got in line. Celie turned to me and said, "Wait until my mother hears I get to carry the flag. And wait until my father hears that I get to sing. . . ."

"And I get to twirl and wear my dance costume. . . ."

"Dance costume? Twirl?" Celie said. "The honor guard just carries a baton."

"I'm going to ask her if it's okay if I twirl it, just once or twice, and she said to dress in something appropriate."

"You're a nut," Celie said. Then she took my hand and shouted, "We're jumping in together."

We jumped into the center of the rope and sang,

"All in together, girls,
How do you like the weather, girls. . . .
I see the teacher, looking out the window. . . ."

Just then Roberta and Peter came out from the cookie room and Roberta said in a real loud voice, "Wouldn't you know the dummies in our class would pick a foreigner to carry the flag and Miss Fatty as the honor guard?"

I stopped jumping and shouted, "I dare you to repeat that. I dare you. Who's a foreigner and who do you think you're calling Miss Fatty?"

Roberta smiled that sneaky smile of hers and said, "If you don't know, Amy, you're the biggest dummy of them all."

I ran over to her, holding up my fist, and said, "Who do you think you're calling a dummy? Just because you've got that dumb belt on, you think you can go around calling people names."

I put my fist down and when I did, she gave me a push. I pushed her back.

"Don't you touch me," she said. "You keep your crummy hands to yourself, Amy, or I swear you'll end up at the end of the whole line." Then she began to scream, "Miss Finnegan! Miss Finnegan! Amy won't keep her hands to herself." She started to run back into the school.

"Miss Finnegan's gone," Celie yelled after her. "Miss Finnegan's gone and nobody else will believe you."

Roberta turned back and shouted, "You just wait. You just wait. I'm telling her first thing tomorrow morning, and then you'll see who'll be honor guard."

Then she took Peter's arm, and the two of them walked to the boys' side of the playground.

I stuck my tongue out at her back and called, "I won't have to see, because it'll be me." But my stomach said something else. Because if Roberta told Miss Finnegan, we both knew who she'd believe.

3

"Don't worry, Amy," Celie said as we started home after school; "you'll get to be honor guard. Bootsy said he'd take care of Roberta. Don't worry."

We walked through the playground and then to the sidewalk that led to the 88's. I didn't answer Celie. I just kept walking, looking down at the pieces of grass growing in between the cracks. That creep, Roberta. She made me feel so bad, calling me Miss Fatty in front of everybody and then calling Celie a foreigner just because her parents spoke Italian. Celie was better than anybody in that whole school. She was the best friend I ever had. Everybody liked Celie. Everybody but Roberta and Miss Finnegan and Peter . . .

"Amy," Celie said, pulling at my arm, "I just remembered I have a singing lesson. Walk with me, will you?"

I shook my head. "Mr. Wood keeps you too long. And besides, he never lets me in. I don't feel like waiting outside today."

"Come on, Amy. Just walk over with me. You don't have to wait. Don't you want to see Count Dracula?" Then she stuck her top teeth way out and pulled back her hair and said, "Walk with me or I will suck out all of your blood."

"Cut it out, Celie. I don't feel like laughing."

"Come with me, then."

"Okay," I said, "but I'm not going to wait for you."

She grabbed my arm and we turned around and raced back through the schoolyard and toward the bridge that led to Mr. Wood's house.

Celie began to slow down when we got to his street. Mr. Wood was standing on his porch, waiting for her. His hair was slicked back and if he'd had a black cape, he would have looked exactly like Dracula. He waved his hand and told Celie to hurry.

"I'll call you when I get home," she said. "Thanks for walking with me."

"That's okay," I said and started home. I walked past the school and when I cut through the tennis courts at the junior high, I saw Robbie near the bicycle stand, helping a girl get a bike out of the rack.

"Robbie, wait up," I shouted.

When he saw me coming, he yanked the bike out of the rack and handed it to the girl. It was Gloreen.

"Wait there, Amy," he called. "I'll be there in a second."

Then he turned back to Gloreen. She was kind of tall and whenever he talked to her, he stood so straight his back looked starched. She was laughing and I heard her say, "See you tomorrow, Robert. See you tomorrow." She always said things twice to him. He put her books in the basket behind the seat and came over to me, took me by the arm, and whispered, "You better not say anything about what your friend Celie told you."

"What do you think I am, a blabbermouth like you? And let go of my arm."

He dropped it and we started home.

We walked through the village, past Buxton's bake-shop, and then started up the 88's. When we got half-way up, I turned to Robbie and said, "Let's sit down for a while."

He usually ran up the 88's two at a time, and I thought he'd tell me I was a pain, but he didn't.

We sat and looked down at the town. I could see the library and the school and the beach. After a while, I told him about moving-up day and what Roberta had said. "Do you think she can make Miss Finnegan take me out?"

He shook his head and said, "If she does, go in to Mr. Mueller and tell him what happened. He's a good guy. Miss Finnegan is an old fart. You think Mr. Muel-ler doesn't know that?"

"But what about Roberta? She's a monitor."

"She's a jerk. Let Bootsy take care of her."

The fire whistle blew, and Robbie looked over at me and said, "Come on, Amy, let's go. It's getting late and I've got to feed the fish."

We started up the stairs, but before we got to the top, he sat down again, and looked down toward town.

"You okay?"

"Just winded," he said, rubbing his legs.

I sat next to him. "It looks nice from up here," he said.

I nodded my head.

"Do you know when I like it best?" he said. "At Christmastime, when all the lights are shining and you can see over to Boston."

"Me, too," I said.

"Remember the Christmas we got Baron and Dad put him in a box under the tree?"

"Yeah," I said. "And remember how I wouldn't believe he was a boy because I wanted a girl?"

"You are *so* weird."

"Next dog is going to be a girl," I said. "Maybe if we ask Momma, she'll let us get a little lady dog."

"I don't want another dog," Robbie said.

"Me neither," I said real fast. But I wasn't telling the truth. I wanted another Baron. One that would be my own and not Robbie's. One that I wouldn't have to visit at Uncle Sam's. I got up and started up the stairs, but Robbie just sat there.

"Are you okay now?"

He nodded, and then started up the stairs.

"I'll race you up," I said.

And for the first time ever, I won.

4

When Robbie and I got home, my mother wasn't there, but there was a note from her on the refrigerator.

Hi — Took the bus to Boston with Dad. Aunt Jane has tickets to the Pops concert and is treating us to dinner. There's plenty of food in frig. Plz clean up. (Amy, this includes you.) Get to bed early. Tomorrow is going to be a busy day.

Love,

Mom

P.S. to Susan — Miss Hurley called from the library. She wants you to work tomorrow afternoon starting at two. Stanley called. You're in charge tonight, but don't let it go to your head. — Don't forget to meet us after Amy's moving-up exercises. Dad's treating us to lunch.

P.S. to Robbie — don't make any elaborate plans for tomorrow. I made an appointment for a camp checkup at 4 with Dr. Shermond and one with Dr. Dana to check your braces. I know — I know — It's

the last day of school, but it's the only day both of
them had two appointments open —

P.S. to Amy — the second appointment is for you at
Dr. Shermond's and Dr. Dana is going to check
your bite again. Don't complain — you need a
checkup for gymnastics if you want to join . . . Mrs.
Breene called to ask what time moving-up exercises
begin. Give her a call after supper.

Love again — there are treats in the pantry — Toll
House cookies!

NO ARGUING!

"Is that stupid?" Robbie said. "The last day of school
and I'm spending it like that." He opened the refrigerator, looked in, then banged it closed.

"Hey, Rob, Amy!" Susan called from upstairs. "Remember what Mom said. Make sure you clean up. You
hear me?"

"We hear you," I yelled back.

I love it when my mother and father go out and
let us make supper. They hardly ever go to Boston
because my father says it's too expensive. But sometimes when he takes his class on a bus trip to a mu-
seum or something, my mother gets to go, and then
the kids in his class come home on the bus with
the other teacher. My father says it's like a half-
free trip because then they only have to pay to get
home.

I made myself two mayonnaise and peanut butter sandwiches, then I poured a big glass of milk and sat on the back porch glider to eat.

Robbie came out with a can of tuna fish and a bottle of grape juice. "How can you eat that?" he said. "It's disgusting. Mom should see you."

It was true. My mother wouldn't let me eat mayonnaise and peanut butter sandwiches because she said there was too much fat in them. She always says things like "Amy, why don't you have a glass of skim milk instead of regular milk?" or "Do you really think you need that cookie?" Stuff like that. She doesn't come right out and say, "You're fat," but I kind of know what she's thinking.

I sat there pushing the glider back and forth and eating the sandwiches, taking little bites so they'd last longer. I sipped the cold milk and let it mix with the mayonnaise and peanut butter. After I was finished, I lay back on the glider and closed my eyes. One more day of school. One more day of Roberta. And Peter. And Miss Finnegan. Miss Finnegan . . .

I slid off the glider and sat down next to Robbie.

"Are you sure Bootsy can take care of Roberta?"

"Sure I'm sure."

"But what if he doesn't?"

"Then I will," he said. "Quit worrying."

I wanted to kiss him, but he hated that, so all I did was say thanks.

I got another glass of milk and went upstairs. Susan was on the telephone with Stanley and I whispered to her, "Can I call Celie?"

She put her hand over the phone and said, "In a minute."

"Don't take all day," I said.

I went into my bedroom, put the milk on my night-stand, and lay on my bed for a while, staring up at the ceiling. My ceiling had swirls all over it and I always tried to find the beginning and the end of the swirls, but I never could. My eyes would go around and around and then I'd get mixed up and the end would look like the beginning and the beginning would look like the end. The only part I was ever really sure of was the center.

After a while, I went out to the hall. Susan was still on the phone.

"Get off," I said. "I want to call Celie."

"In a minute."

"You said that before, and you've been talking for an hour. I'm going over to Celie's, and if Momma gets mad, I'll tell her it was your fault." Before Susan could answer me, I was down the stairs and out the door.

I took the shortcut through the field to get to Celie's house. I started to run, and when I did, the grass bent down and the bugs began to fly all over. One went up my nose and some went up my legs. But I kept running.

"Hi, Jemma," I called to Celie's sister. "Where's Celie?"

"She's still over at Mr. Wood's. He wants her to practice the song she's going to sing tomorrow."

"She coming back soon?"

"I don't know. She called my mother a little while ago and told her she tried to call you —"

"Susan's talking to Stanley."

"— to tell you about the puppies. . . ."

"Puppies? Puppies? . . . Who's got puppies?"

"Mr. Wood's sister. The one who just moved upstairs from him and —"

But before she could finish, I raced down the street. I ran until I could hardly breathe and then I walked as fast as I could until I got to Mr. Wood's house. Celie was standing on the porch; Gloreen was beside her. When Celie saw me, she shouted, "Hurry up. I tried to call you fifty times."

I ran up the stairs, pushed the gate open, and hurried over to the side of the porch. There was a mother dog in a box with six little puppies.

I knelt beside them and put my face right next to the box to look at them. They were so cute I wanted to pick them all up and squeeze them. They were all pushing to get near their mother and they were making little squeaky sounds. They smelled like the fresh straw Uncle Sam puts in Elmer and Sari's stalls.

"Don't touch them now, dear. Wait until they've finished their feeding," Mr. Wood's sister said, wiping her hands on her apron.

"I'll wait," I said. "I'll wait." I already knew which one I wanted. She was cute and sweet with a curled-up tail, and she was the only one who wasn't pushing to get to her mother. She just waited until it was her turn to eat. When they finished, I put my hands into the box and took her. She was the smallest, furriest, blackest one. I held her real close to me and whispered, "You're mine, Samantha, and I'm going to come and get you as soon as I can."

She felt soft and warm, but her nose was a small black grape, all cold and wet, and when I kissed it, it felt like my father's kisses when he has shaving cream all over his face. I held her for a long time, and when it was time to put her back, I said, "Can I buy this one?"

"You don't have to buy one," the lady said. "I'm looking for good homes for them. Is that the one you want?"

I hugged Samantha harder. "Yes," I said. "This is the one I want." I loved her already.

Gloreen knelt beside me and picked up a puppy who looked exactly like Samantha and said, "This is mine. My brother wanted that one," she said, pointing to one that was running all over the box, "but my mother said this one is more ladylike."

"That's why I like this one," I said. And I hugged Samantha again.

"They won't be ready to leave their mother for another week or so," Mr. Wood's sister said. "You make sure your mother says it's all right."

She asked me for my name and address and said, "I'll call you when they're ready to leave their mother."

"I'll come to visit her," I said. "I'll help you clean up and everything."

She smiled and said that would be fine with her. "Better get on home now."

I hugged Samantha for the last time and gave her a

kiss. She smelled better than sawdust. She smelled like the geraniums my mother always plants in the backyard.

"See you tomorrow," I said. And then I put her back in the box right next to her mother.

"Come on, Amy. I'm starved," Celie said. "I want to get home."

I waved good-bye to Samantha and thanked Mr. Wood's sister. Gloreen told me to say hello to Robert. Two times. I was so excited I had to go to the bathroom, but I was afraid to ask Mr. Wood, and I didn't want to bother his sister.

"Could somebody burst if they didn't pee, Celie?"

"You'd better not let your father hear you say pee. 'It's urinate, Amy,' " she said, imitating my father. "The word is *urinate*."

"But can somebody burst?"

"How would I know? But I'll bet Roberta will burst when she hears what Bootsy knows about her. . . ."

"What does Bootsy know about her?"

"Never mind. You'll see," she said. "And you know what? There were only three kids who said they'd tell Miss Finnegan what really happened."

"Who were the three kids?"

"Me, Bootsy, and Patrick."

"But Marilyn saw what happened. Why didn't she say she would?"

Celie stopped walking and took my arm and said, "Amy, grow up. If you don't get to be an honor guard, who gets to do it all by herself?"

"She does," I said.

"Right," Celie said. "And do you think she cares that you won't?"

"Maybe she'll change her mind."

"Yeah," Celie said, "and maybe Bootsy will use a handkerchief."

We ran the rest of the way home, and when I left Celie, I cut through the field and into my yard. I pushed the screen door open and burst into the kitchen. Susan was sitting at the table reading a movie magazine and Robbie was making a sandwich. I flopped in the chair beside Susan. "You've got to see the puppies I just saw at Mr. Wood's house," I said. "They're so cute I could take them all."

She nodded her head and kept reading.

"I picked one out already."

"Amy," Susan said, "you know how Mom feels about another dog."

"Yeah, but if we —"

"How many times do I have to tell you. I don't want another dog," Robbie said, pushing a piece of bologna into his mouth. "I've got Baron."

"But it would be like having a little Baron, only she'd be here instead of at Uncle Sam's."

"I don't care where Baron is," he said, biting into the sandwich so hard some mustard flew out and plopped on the table. "He's still Baron."

"I know that," I said, "but . . ."

"I don't want a new dog," he said, wiping up the mustard with his fingers and then licking them off.

I turned to Susan and said, "Sue, you should see this puppy. She's so cute. She's black and little and she's got a sweet black nose and she looked at me and I could tell she was smiling. She licked my face, and do you know what?"

"No, what?" she said.

"She's for free. The lady is giving them away. For free, Sue."

Susan put the movie magazine on the table and pointed to an ad that said, "Do you want to be a movie star?" Then she looked at me and said, "You've got about as much chance of getting another dog as I do of being a star."

"But if we all say we want it, Momma will say yes."

"Come on," Sue said; "that's how we got Baron and look what happened to him."

"That's because we never asked how big he was going to get. I asked already and the lady said as big as a cocker spaniel. Please, Sue, tell Momma you want her. Please."

She picked up the magazine and said, "Sure, Amy. But I know what the answer is going to be."

I gave her a hug and then turned to Rob and said, "Rob, please. Baron would have a sister, just like Elmer and Sari. Please. Momma will definitely say yes if we all nag her."

He shook his head and gulped the rest of his juice down.

"Gloreen was there tonight. She's taking one. They'd be cousins."

"Don't you ever give up?" he said. "I told you no."

I started out of the kitchen, but Sue called me back

and said, "Remember what Mom said. You clean up your own mess." Then she went into the living room. "Hi, Stanley," I heard her say, "I just read about the best movie. *The Treasure of the Sierra Madre.* Humphrey Bogart plays the part of . . ."

"Don't take forever," I yelled. "Momma told me to call Mrs. Breene."

After I cleaned up, I remembered my mother had said there were Toll House cookies. I took some and went back upstairs. "Want some cookies, Rob?" I yelled as I went by his room. I poked my head in and held out my hand. "Have some."

He shook his head.

"You feeling okay? They're Toll House."

"I ate too much bologna."

I started to eat another cookie. There were exactly three chocolate pieces in it. "Do you know what I'm going to do when I get married?" I said.

Robbie didn't answer me.

"I'm going to make Toll House cookies with a hundred chocolate pieces in each cookie, and then I'm going to sit down and eat them all myself."

I went into my room, got undressed, and climbed into bed. I closed my eyes and saw Samantha. So cute and so black and so furry. I could hardly wait to take her home. I could sleep with her every night.

I decided to write my mother a note about Samantha. Maybe if I wrote that we missed Baron so much and summer was here, she'd feel sorry and I wouldn't have to nag her so much for her to say yes. I reached over to my night table to get some paper and when I did, the glass of milk spilled onto my nightgown and all over my bed. I hated the stinky smell of milk when it soaked into my clothes. "Yuck!" I yelled and I tore off my nightgown and ran down the hall in my underpants, hoping Robbie wouldn't come out of his room. I went into the linen closet and wrapped a towel around me.

The linen closet is just about the best place in the house. It's like a little room. My mother told me it was a maid's room, but we never had a maid, so she uses it for linen and sewing. I got the sheets down from the shelf, but before I left, I could hear Susan laughing through the register on the floor. That's why the linen closet is the best place. You can hear people talking in the living room. I heard Susan say, "Me, too, Stanley. I love foreign films." Sometimes she talked so stupid.

Once when I was in the linen closet, writing in my diary, I heard my father tell my mother that he loved to watch her running toward him because he liked to see her bounce. Like my mother was a ball or something. And then my mother said in a funny voice, "Oh, Bob, stop." Sometimes I think they talk stupider than Susan does.

After I changed my bed, I started the note to my mother, but then I remembered I was supposed to call Mrs. Breene. "Get off the phone," I yelled down to Susan. When she finally did, I called. Mr. Breene answered and said in his grouchy voice, "She ain't home." I asked him to give her a message, but he said, "I'm no secketary."

Dear Momma:

I saw the cutest puppy today. For free. Celie's singing teacher's sister has six. Sue said she'd love to have one. I know Robbie would, too. Momma, I picked out a real quiet one. She'll be a little lady Baron. And the lady said she'd stay really small. Not like poor Baron. Please, Momma. Please say yes.

Love,

Amy

P.S. Moving-up exercises start at 11 and guess who gets to be honor guard? ME. That's who — I hope. Miss Finnegan invited the junior high kids, so Robbie gets to see me, too. Mrs. Breene wasn't home and Mr. Breene said he was nooo secketary. Could you call her tomorrow?

Love,

ME

X O X O X O X O

P.P.S. Please don't say no.

I tried to sleep but I couldn't. I kept thinking about Samantha and about Roberta. After a while, my eyes got tired, and I pulled the covers up around me and turned toward the open window. The moon was shining through my curtains, and I looked up and said, "God, please let my mother say yes about the dog. And please, if you can, could you make Roberta very late for school? Like after the assembly is over. Please, God. Please."

5

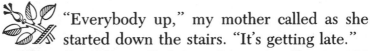 "Everybody up," my mother called as she started down the stairs. "It's getting late."

"Mom," Robbie called from his room, "how could you do this to me? The last day of school, and you make an appointment with the doctor."

"Can't be helped . . . besides, it's not until four. You've got most of the day."

"Ellen, where's my razor?" my father called from the bathroom.

"In the shower."

"Why do you have to use my razor?"

"Momma, did you see my note?"

"We'll talk about it when you come down, Amy."

I slid out of bed and onto the floor and put on my socks and sneakers. I got into my last-day-of-school dress, which was as stupid-looking as the plaid one, and ran down the hall to the bathroom.

"Robbie," my mother called from the bottom of the stairs, "I left two bottles on the bathroom shelf. Get a urine specimen. Dr. Shermond has to check it for your camp physical. Tell Amy to get one, too."

"I hear you," I yelled.

Sometimes I couldn't understand my mother at all.

She always said things like that were private and you shouldn't go talking about it all over the place, and here she was screaming it for everybody to hear.

I went into the bathroom, washed up, and brushed my teeth, and made sure that I got the specimen into the little bottle, which was very hard work.

I thought about Robbie going to camp. Usually I hated it when Robbie went to camp, even if it was just for two weeks. But this time I didn't think I'd miss him because I'd have Samantha all to myself and Momma and Daddy, too. Susan was always at the library or talking to Stanley.

I didn't like to go away from home. I liked everything to be the same. I didn't even like to go to day camp, and my mother had to get Mrs. Breene to come over if she was at the hospital and my father had summer classes.

Once I went to stay with Aunt Emma for a week and I got so homesick Uncle Sam had to take me home the first night at one o'clock in the morning. "Now, Sam, put your teeth in and stop that cussing," Aunt Emma said. "She's only nine and she misses her mother."

Uncle Sam put his teeth in, pulled his hat on his head, yanked his jacket off the hook, and started down to the barn to get the truck. He stopped cussing and called back over his shoulder, "Well, she'll be twenty-nine before she gets to stay out here without her momma, I can tell you that." That was all right with me because I didn't like to do it anyway.

"Amy! AMY!" I heard Susan yelling as she banged

on the door. "You're not the only one who has to get ready. Get out of there. Now."

"Okay. Okay," I said. "I'm coming right out."

I put the specimen bottle back on the shelf and went down to breakfast.

"Momma, did you read the note?"

She nodded her head and came over to the table and sat down. "I'm so glad you're going to be an honor guard," she said, pouring herself another cup of coffee. "Mrs. Breene can't come. She said something about having to help Mr. Breene with the tomato plants. But she said she'll be thinking about you."

I wet my finger and picked up the Cheerios I'd spilled out of the box.

"Did you read the part about the little lady puppy? She's so sweet, and Mr. Wood's sister said they're for free. For free, Momma. And she's so cute, it'll be just like having a little Baron."

"We'll talk about it later." She put one hand at the end of the table and swept the rest of the Cheerios off with her other hand. "You'd better get going, Amy. Miss Finnegan won't appreciate your being late."

When I got outside, I looked up at the sky and said, "Thank you, God. At least she didn't say no."

6

I ran all the way to the 88's, but Celie wasn't there. I waited for a while and then raced down the stairs and into the schoolyard. All the kids were there, and Bootsy and Celie and Patrick were talking to Marilyn.

I called and ran toward them.

"Amy," Roberta yelled. "Hey, Amy, stop running or I'll report you to Miss Finnegan."

I didn't stop, and when I got over to Bootsy and Celie, I heard Bootsy say to Marilyn, "Either you tell Roberta you're not backing her up with Fartso Finnegan, or I'm going to tell your mother I saw you smoking in the movies."

Marilyn looked at him and said, "I never smoked in the movies." Then she turned to Celie and said, "You know I never smoked in the movies."

Celie shrugged her shoulders. "Bootsy's the one who saw you."

Marilyn looked over at Patrick. "Bootsy doesn't lie," he said.

And Bootsy never did. But Marilyn never smoked.

"Hey, Amy . . . ," Bootsy said when he saw me,

"everything's great." Then he turned to Marilyn and said, "You ready? There's Roberta now."

Marilyn didn't say anything, but when she looked at me, she put her baton behind her back.

"Come on, you guys," Bootsy said, "we're going to fix her real good. Right, Marilyn?"

Marilyn swallowed hard, but she nodded her head. I could have kissed Bootsy.

"It's time to form the lines," Roberta said. "No fooling around. Boys in the boys' line. Girls in the girls'."

"Hey, Roberta," Bootsy called, "do you know my friends, Celie and Amy?"

Roberta turned around and said, "That means you, too, Russell. Get in line."

"Well, maybe I should introduce you. This is Celie and this is Amy," he said, putting his hand first on Celie's shoulder and then on mine. "And if you don't say you're sorry you called Celie a foreigner, and if you don't shut up about Amy pushing you, guess what Celie's going to do?"

"Get in line," Roberta said, "or you'll end up in detention."

"Tell her, Celie," Bootsy said.

Celie walked over to Roberta, put her hands on her hips, and said, "I'm going to tell Miss Finnegan I saw you sneak into the boys' bathroom and peek under one of the doors. I saw you, Roberta, and I'll tell."

Roberta's face got red. She leaned over to Celie and said in a loud whisper, "I never did any such thing. You're a rotten liar."

I tapped Roberta's shoulder and said, "And if you

don't say you're sorry you called Celie a foreigner, I'm going to tell her I was with Celie when she saw you." I really wasn't. But Celie never, ever lied about anything to anybody, so it was almost like being there.

"Shut up, Amy," Roberta said, pulling on her stupid monitor's belt. "You're nothing but a big baby. You'd swear to anything she said."

"You won't have that belt next year, so you'd better stop pushing everybody around," I said, feeling very brave with Bootsy and Patrick and Celie beside me.

The last bell rang and Roberta told everybody to get in line again, but Patrick ran in front of her and said, "Roberta, if you start something with Miss Finnegan, I'm the one you looked at in the boys' room, and if you don't think I'll tell her, you're crazy."

Roberta looked as if she was going to cry. I didn't feel sorry for her. I always felt sorry when anybody cried, especially in school. But not Roberta. She was always making trouble and then she'd act real sweet, like she didn't know what the trouble was all about.

Bootsy took Marilyn by the arm and stood in front of Roberta. "You don't have Marilyn on your side, either. Does she, Marilyn?"

Marilyn shook her head and burst into tears.

Roberta looked toward the boys' playground. "You can forget Peter, too," Bootsy said. "I called him last night and told him if he didn't shut up, I'd tell Miss Finnegan he was the one who wrote 'Miss Finnegan got some gin again and did some sin again,' in the boys' playground."

He turned to me and winked. "I saw it there again this morning."

Roberta's face got real red and her eyes got all glassy-looking.

"Okay," she said, "you win this time. But you haven't heard the end of this, Amy Martin. And neither have you, Celie DiCarlo."

I held up my hands and shook my fists the way boxers do when they win a fight. Celie slapped me on the back and Bootsy pulled me into the line. With his right hand. But I didn't care. And when it was time to file into school, I swung his arm back and forth and didn't let it go until we got into the classroom.

"Ladies and gentlemen, good morning," Miss Finnegan said. "Let's get on with what must be done before the program begins. Take everything out of your desks."

"Miss Finnegan, what do you want us to do with the inkwells?"

"Leave them exactly where they are. Mr. Tirrell will attend to them later."

"Miss Finnegan, there are ants in my desk."

"Peter, get Mr. Tirrell."

"Yes, Miss Finnegan."

"Patrick, get your speech and practice in the cloak-room."

"Yes, Miss Finnegan."

"Miss Finnegan, somebody stepped on my glasses."

"Roberta, take Edith to the nurse."

"Yes, Miss Finnegan, I'll be happy to."

"Dear Lord," said Miss Finnegan as she slumped into her chair, "I'll be glad to see the end of this day."

After we'd finished cleaning the desks and all the books had been put away and the blackboards had been cleaned and it was finally time for the exercises to begin, I got my toe shoes and my dance costume from under my desk and went to the girls' bathroom to change.

I picked the biggest stall and sat on the toilet to put my tights and my toe shoes on. I loved ballet. Miss Eckman once told my mother that I wasn't quite built for ballet, but my mother told her it would be good exercise. "It will help her slim down."

I pulled my tights up and then put on my leotard and my skirt. I loved my costume. It had a yellow net skirt that stuck way out, and when I put on my black tights and leotard and spun around, I looked like a black-and-yellow top.

I stood on my toes and twirled around in the toilet, then I pushed the door open and began to dance around in the girls' room. I danced all the time at home. I'd pretend I was grown-up and on a real stage and I was tall and skinny and a handsome boy would pick me up and run around the stage with me. I would point my toes, the way Miss Eckman told me to, and then he would put me down and spin me around and around.

"Ladies. Ladies . . . , come out of there and back to the class," Miss Finnegan called. "The program is about to begin."

I ran as fast as I could on my toes back to the classroom and grabbed my baton.

"Get in line, ladies and —" and then Miss Finnegan pointed her finger at me, her eyes wide behind her glasses, and said, "and just where do you think you're going in that outfit?"

"But, Miss Finnegan, you said to wear . . ."

"Don't but-Miss-Finnegan me. Does your mother know that this is what you consider appropriate attire for honor guard?"

I shook my head.

"Well, get yourself back into your dress and shoes this instant."

"But I wore sneakers. . . ."

"Then struggle in those . . . those *things* the best you can. But stay off your toes."

It was hard to wear toe shoes and not be on your toes, but I changed into my dress and took my place in line.

"Cecelia, get behind the band and don't poke anyone with the flag," Miss Finnegan said. "And remember when the band plays 'God Bless America,' that is your cue to begin singing the school anthem."

She walked up and down, pointing to each kid as she spoke.

"Theodore and Timothy, pick up the banner and see that it doesn't drag on the floor."

Bootsy and Tim lifted the banner so high, all I could see of them was their hair.

"Theodore, tie your shoe."

Bootsy put his side of the banner on the floor and started to tie his shoe.

"What did I tell you about dragging the school banner on the floor?"

Bootsy picked up his side of the banner.

"Patrick, are you ready?"

Patrick held up his speech.

"Amory? Marilyn? Are you two all set? And Amory, please be careful with that baton."

I held the baton until my knuckles turned white.

"And now," Miss Finnegan said, holding up her hands, "all of you give me your undivided attention. As soon as Cecelia begins to sing the anthem, everyone is to march forward. Now we will all march in place. Let's keep time. . . ."

Miss Finnegan clapped and marched in place, raising her feet high, her Minnie Mouse shoes keeping time. When Miss Finnegan turned around, I got up on my toes so high I was taller than Bootsy and held my baton in front of me. Bootsy and Tim stretched the banner way out. And then the band began to play "God Bless America" and Celie began to sing:

> *"God bless our splendid school,*
> *School that we love . . ."*

I looked over at Miss Finnegan to make sure she wasn't looking, then I twirled my baton just the way Miss Eckman had taught me and marched in time to Celie's voice —

"Bless our teachers
who guide us
through the years
always cheering us on . . ."

Miss Finnegan hissed at me, and I put the baton on my shoulder, got off my toes, and kept marching.

"From the first grade
to the third grade,
then the fifth grade . . ."

My ankles hurt, but I kept marching.

"on and on . . .
God bless the Franklin School,
our splendid school . . ."

Marilyn's baton hit me on the back of the head, but I didn't miss a step.

"God bless the Franklin School,
our splendid school."

The band stopped playing, and Miss Finnegan ushered everybody onto the stage, except Bootsy and Tim and Celie. Mr. Mueller said good morning and told us to take our seats and then asked Miss Finnegan to lead the banner bearers and the flag bearer on stage. Poor Bootsy. He should have tied his shoe. He got up to the second step, then his lacing got stuck and he fell up the stairs, knocking Tim down with him. They looked so funny. Bootsy was lying across the stage and Tim was pinned against the piano with his end of the banner.

"What did I tell you about those laces, Theodore?" Miss Finnegan said through clenched teeth.

I felt so bad for Bootsy because the kids started to laugh and some of the people in the audience had their hands up to their mouths, trying not to.

Mr. Mueller ran over, picked up the banner, and helped Tim and Bootsy up. "These things happen," he said in a cheerful voice. Then he turned to the audience and said, "Bear with us for another moment or two and then we'll get on with the festivities."

When everything settled down, Celie came on stage with the flag and Patrick led us in the salute to the flag and we all sang the "Star Spangled Banner."

"That was wonderful. Simply wonderful," Mr. Mueller said, motioning for everybody to sit down. "And now, parents, teachers, students, and friends, welcome to the moving-up exercises of the Franklin School. . . ."

A big fly flew around Mr. Mueller, and after a long time landed right on top of his head. It looked like a barrette, only Mr. Mueller didn't have any hair to hold.

". . . I can remember when I was a lad about to enter sixth grade," Mr. Mueller went on. "I was a bit . . ."

The fly stayed on top of his head for a while and then it flew up toward the ceiling, looking as though it were playing tag with the dust floating down. I watched it until I couldn't see it anymore.

". . . and now," I could hear Mr. Mueller say, "it is my pleasure to turn the program over to Patrick Youngs."

Patrick shook hands with Mr. Mueller and began his speech. He began it about five times.

I started to get real fidgety. I stretched my arms. Then I stretched my legs out, and when I did, my baton rolled off my lap. I picked it up and sneaked a look at Miss Finnegan. She was whispering something in Roberta's ear. Roberta poked Marilyn, who poked Carol, who poked me in the ribs and said, "Miss Finnegan says to sit still or you'll be spending the afternoon with her."

That did it. I sat still.

". . . Thank you very much, Patrick," Mr. Mueller said. "That was an inspiring talk and one that your classmates will remember for a long, long time. And now, boys and girls, let's start up the band and march into summer."

"Well, ladies and gentlemen," Miss Finnegan said when we got back to the classroom, "consider yourselves sixth graders. Come down to visit me often next term."

Was she serious? Nobody answered except Roberta, who said in that disgusting voice of hers, "I'll come down very often, Miss Finnegan. I'm going to miss you very much."

I almost threw up.

"Did you ask your mother if you can come to lunch with us?" I called to Celie.

"It's fine with her," she said.

"Come on, then. What are we waiting for?"

As soon as I saw Robbie, I shouted, "Wasn't I good? I kept time all the way."

"You looked like an idiot in those shoes," Robbie said.

"I did?"

"You did."

"Well, probably nobody noticed but you."

My father put his arm around my shoulder and said, "You did just fine. You and Celie were great."

My mother tried to smooth down my bangs. "You were, Amy," she said. "You, too, Celie." And then she said, "We'd better get going. Susan's meeting us at Nino's at noon."

The last day of school and birthdays were the only days my mother didn't complain about us eating pizza and drinking soda. She even let us order a pizza with the works and she didn't say, "Why don't you have milk instead of another Coke?"

When we'd finished eating, I looked over at my mother with a sad expression on my face and said, "Momma, did you think about the dog? Please, please, let me have her. I'll do everything. You won't have to do anything. She can't leave her mother for a while and I'll get everything ready. I promise."

My mother looked over at my father. He shrugged and looked over at me. She looked back at me and said, "You know I'm working at least two days a week this summer and Daddy's got classes. I don't think it's fair to Mrs. Breene to put up with a puppy who isn't trained."

"But, Momma," I said, "when I called the lady yesterday to tell her you'd probably say yes, she told me they'd be all cleaned when they leave their mother. She said that, Momma. You can ask her yourself."

"Cleaned? That's not possible. Puppies can't possibly be trained in six weeks."

"She probably said weaned," Susan said. "Not cleaned."

"What's that?"

"That's when the puppies don't need their mother's milk," my mother said. "It doesn't mean they'll be trained."

"I'll train her, Momma. I really will."

My mother sighed and looked back at my father and said, "What do you think?"

"Give her a chance. She'll do it. Right, Amy?"

I squeezed his neck so hard, he began to cough. Then I ran over and kissed my mother. "Come on, Celie, let's go over to see them." Then I said in a real quiet voice, "Robbie, do you want to come? Gloreen probably will be there."

He shook his head.

"You sure?"

"I can see her anytime," he said.

Celie and I raced to the door.

"Make sure you're back home no later than three-thirty," my mother called after us. "The doctor's appointment is at four."

"I will."

"Three-thirty, sharp."

When we got to the door, I heard Robbie call, "Wait up, Ame. Maybe I will go."

And I was so sure then that this would be the best summer I ever had.

7

Dr. Shermond had been our doctor for so long that I never knew there were any other doctors in Manuet. He was small and skinny and his hair was so short it looked like grass when it's just been cut. Robbie called him Flattop, like the gangster in his Dick Tracy comic books. But Dr. Shermond's hair wasn't like Flattop's. It was mostly white with about five red hairs sticking out on top.

"Amy," he'd say, "if you get any bigger, you're going to be able to eat off the top of my head." And then he'd look at me and expect me to laugh, but it wasn't funny because I'd heard it at least ninety-five times before.

But he tried to be real nice, and when he was finished examining me, he'd tell me to help myself to a balloon. "A balloon?" I said to my mother the last time. "What does he think I am, five years old or something?"

We got to his office right at four o'clock, but it was crowded. Robbie and I began to read the comic books. After a long time, the nurse called Robbie's name, and he went in. My mother motioned to me to come and sit beside her. She was looking through a magazine that had bathing suits in it. "How do you like this suit,

Amy?" she asked. "You'll be needing a new one this year."

"What's the matter with the ones I had last year?"

"Didn't you tell me all the girls had two-piece suits last year and you were tired of looking like a baby?"

It was true. I did look like a baby next to some of the girls. Marilyn had breasts. Even Celie had a little. But I was flat. "You're almost a year younger than most of the girls in your class," my mother had said when I complained to her. "You'll catch up." But that didn't help.

"Do you like this one?" she said, pointing to one with a top that had a real pointy front.

"Yuck," I said. "I'd rather wear last year's. That looks disgusting."

My mother closed the magazine and reached for another and said, "Okay, Amy, but you'd better try them on first. They might be tight."

I started to say something but when I looked over at her, she had the magazine opened to one of those stupid stories: "Love on a Rainy Afternoon." I couldn't believe my mother would read that junk.

Robbie was in the doctor's office for a long time. Usually it took Dr. Shermond about fifteen minutes to examine us and then the nurse would come out and call my mother in. After a while, my mother got up and went over to the secretary to ask what was taking so long. "He's probably talking baseball to Robbie," she said, "but I'll go check."

"Not too much longer," she said, coming out of the doctor's office. "The doctor's just about finished."

My mother picked up another magazine, but she didn't read it. She kept looking over at the door to the examining room.

"Momma," I said, "Mr. Wood's sister said I probably could take Samantha home next week. Maybe Thursday. Did you hear me, Momma?"

"Yes, Amy."

"Can I get her bed ready?"

"I suppose so," she said.

Robbie finally came out of Dr. Shermond's office and when he did, the nurse asked my mother to go in. She was in there for a long time and when she came out, I went in. Dr. Shermond told me how tall I was getting and how I probably could eat off the top of his head, but he didn't talk too much after that.

As soon as I came out, my mother went back into his office. She was in there for a while and when she came out, Dr. Shermond was with her. "Don't worry, Ellen," he said. "I just want to check things out." Then he put his arm around her and said, "I'll have the results back in five or six days."

"You'll call me just as soon as you do?" my mother said.

"Just as soon as I do," he said. And then looking over at Robbie and me, he said, "Don't forget your balloons, you two."

"It must have been mobbed in there," my father said as we got into the car. "I thought I'd be late picking you up. What time is the appointment with Dr. Dana?"

My mother took a deep breath and said, "Oh, God . . . I forgot about him. We were supposed to be there ten minutes ago. I'm too tired, Bob. I think I'll call him and make an appointment for next week."

"Whew," I said, as I fell into the back seat, "am I glad for that."

"You take it easy," my father said to my mother. "I'll cook. Do we have any charcoal?"

"I'm not sure," she said.

"Maybe we'd better stop at the A&P," he said. "What do you feel like having?"

"You decide," she said.

"How about steak?"

"Fine."

"Hey, Dad, hold up," Robbie said when we passed the junior high school. "I've got to pick up my bike."

I poked him and said, "Yes, Robert, you have to pick up your bike. You have to pick up your bike."

He gave me a shove and got out of the car.

"Be home soon," my father called after him.

Before my mother and I went into the store, I asked her if I could get some cereal. Usually she'd tell me, "No sweet cereal. I don't care what the box top is offering." But today she didn't say anything. She sort of walked around putting things in the basket, thinking about something else.

It took a while for her to finish, and when we finally got home, Robbie was putting his bike in the garage.

"Can you help me get Baron's bed down for Samantha?" I called to him.

"Samantha?" he yelled. "Who do you think you're calling Samantha?"

He put his bike in the rack and said, "Didn't I tell

you that *she* is a *he?* Gloreen got the only female. Gloreen wanted a she and she knew how to pick a she. You picked a *he*. A *he*. Not a she."

"Who cares what you say? She's Samantha."

"You're crazy. Anybody with half a brain wouldn't name a he Samantha."

"Are you saying I only have half a brain?"

He looked at me with one of his looks and said, "Don't flatter yourself," and walked toward the house.

"Are you going to help me or not?"

He didn't answer, so I climbed up the ladder and pulled down the old wicker basket Baron had slept in when he was a puppy. He had only fit into it for about a month and then we had to get him a real big one. I brushed off the spider webs. They went over my hands and onto my fingers and looked like the lacy curtains in my mother's bedroom. Then I got a pail of water and some soap and began to scrub.

After a while, Robbie came out of the house and sat on the glider looking around the yard. After a long minute, he walked over to me and said, "You want to go out to see Baron with me and Sue on Sunday? Dad said he'll drive us."

"Sure," I said.

Then he went into the garage and climbed up the ladder and started to pull something down from the eaves. "Maybe I'll finish the doghouse I started for Baron," he said. "The one he got too big for before I finished sanding the wood."

He handed me some lumber and part of a roof. "I called Uncle Sam just now," he said.

"What did he say?"

Robbie stood for a while on the ladder, not saying anything. And then he looked right at me and said, "He says Baron's happy."

He passed me more lumber and then started down the ladder, stopping at the last step. "He said he's really happy."

Then he knelt beside the lumber and began to measure the boards, using his hands to mark off the lengths.

". . . I'll help you with it, Rob."

"Real help or fool-around help?"

"Real help."

I emptied the bucket and put the basket on the porch to dry, then went back to where Robbie was working.

"Okay, I'm ready," I said.

"Here," he said, passing me some sandpaper, "start sanding."

"Sanding? How come I get to do all the dirty work?"

"It's not dirty work. . . ."

"Well, I'm not doing it," I said. I always got the jobs nobody wanted. The only good job I got was at Christmas, when my father lifted me up so I could put the angel on top of the tree. And last year my father had trouble lifting me up, so I'll probably lose that job, too.

"It's clean work. You won't even get your hands dirty."

"That's what you say."

"Forget it, then. I'll do it myself," Robbie said.

"You'd probably do a lousy job anyway. The dog would end up feeling like he was sitting on cactus. . . ."

"Where's the sandpaper?" I said. "You'll see. I won't leave one splinter in it. Not one."

Robbie smiled and handed me the sandpaper.

My father was in the kitchen and when I saw the steam coming from the window over the sink, I knew he was cooling off macaroni he'd boiled for salad. He made the best macaroni salad in the world. He'd put the cooled macaroni into a big bowl with lots of mayonnaise and a little vinegar and chopped olives.

He came outside and soon the smell of charcoal and steak and fat spattering from the grill filled the yard.

"Come on, you two," my mother called. "Come in and wash up. Supper's almost ready."

The picnic table was covered with a yellow tablecloth and my mother had set the table with the summer dishes. It looked like a real party. Only my mother didn't look like she was having fun.

"What's the matter, Momma?"

"Nothing. I'm just tired . . . you go in and get washed."

I ate so much macaroni salad and steak my stomach hurt. When it was time for dessert, Susan brought out the cake and cut each of us a big piece. Usually my mother and father had dessert and coffee in the living room, but tonight was different. The cake was still warm, and some of the frosting dripped down the sides and filled the rim of the cake dish. It was chocolate frosting. Robbie's favorite.

My mother didn't eat much of hers. "Guess I ate too much steak," she said, as she started to clear off the table. "Dad and I will clean up. You kids can take the night off."

Susan called Stanley, and Robbie and I went back to the garage and I started to sand again. I kept getting splinters, and after I had yelled "Ow" a hundred times, Robbie took the sandpaper, wrapped it around a piece of wood, handed it back to me, and said, "You sand with the paper, not your fingers."

"Come on," my mother called, just as I started to sand again, "you've got the whole summer for that. Rob, you too. You look tired."

I dropped the sandpaper and raced toward the house. Robbie yelled after me to help him clean up, but I pretended I didn't hear. I ran in the back door, and when the screen door slammed behind me, I knew it really was summer.

"Thanks for helping, Amy. Thanks a lot," Robbie said when he passed my room. "You sanded at least two inches of board."

"But there are no splinters. I'll do more tomorrow. I promise."

"Anything would be more than you did today," he said. "I want to finish it up so I can paint it before I leave for camp."

"I can paint it while you're gone," I said, as I tried to get a knot out of my sneaker lacing. "I can paint it yellow. Wouldn't that be great?"

"Yellow? Are you serious? I'm the one who started

this for Baron and it was going to be blue. And if you want me to finish it for Sam, it's going to be blue."

"I'm the one who found this dog, Robbie, and don't forget it," I said, and I bit the knot off the lacing and got into bed.

I lay back on my bed, thinking about Samantha. Then I remembered the pillow for Baron's old bed was in the linen closet. The pillow was lying on the floor near the register and when I picked it up, I heard someone crying. I listened real hard and then I realized it was my mother. I got down on the floor and put my head next to the grate.

"Ellen," I heard my father say, "you're jumping to conclusions. Dr. Shermond drew a little blood. He'll have it tested down at the hospital, and it will turn out fine."

His voice was very gentle, but my mother kept crying. Then I heard her say, "But why would Dr. Shermond want to check Rob's white count unless he suspects it might be high? And why would he ask me if Rob's been tired?"

She stopped and I could hear her sob. "And, Bob," she said, "how could I have missed those bruises on his legs?"

"Kids get bruises. They get bruises all the time. Don't you remember when Susan was anemic? She was just about Rob's age. . . ."

"That was her period. I give them vitamins and Rob eats well," she said. "I'm supposed to know all those things."

It got very quiet for a long time and all I could hear was my mother's soft crying.

"Don't do this to yourself, sweetheart. You're letting youself get carried away. Come on, Ellen, drink your coffee. Better yet, I'll get you a little brandy."

I got up from the floor and started back to my room. Dumb old doctor making my mother so upset. I didn't like him anymore. I put Baron's pillow next to me and turned and looked out the window. I thought of what my mother had said about Robbie's blood probably having a lot of white in it. Stupid old doctor. Robbie's blood was just as red as mine.

8

The best part about summer vacation is waking up and remembering that you don't have to go to school. And today was going to the best day of my whole vacation. Today I was going to get Samantha. I was going to take her home. She'd be mine. Really mine.

The house was very quiet, and outside, the only sound came from the tree by my window, where two squirrels ran around the branches. The leaves whispered and whooshed. I watched until one of the squirrels ran down the tree, across the lawn, and out of the yard. The other one disappeared into the very top of the tree. I got dressed and walked softly down the hall to the bathroom. I looked in the mirror and smiled. I sat up on the sink and brushed my teeth and smiled again.

I tiptoed downstairs and went into the pantry and opened the freezer, looking for some leftover cake. When I found it, I cut a big piece and ate it. It was delicious. "How can you eat frozen cake?" my mother would say. "And don't you know cake isn't to be eaten for breakfast?"

I loved frozen cake. And besides, it was made of eggs and flour and milk and chocolate, so it was as good as scrambled eggs, toast, and hot chocolate.

I went down to the basement and got my old doll carriage. It was dusty, and the wheels were rusted and the mattress was stained, but Samantha wouldn't mind. I cleaned it up real fast. Then I pulled it up the stairs and wheeled it out to the front porch.

"Amy," I could hear my mother calling from the kitchen, "come and eat breakfast."

When I went into the kitchen, Robbie was sitting at the table, eating his breakfast and reading the cereal box. Susan was cutting her grapefruit. The juice squirted out and hit the part of the box that said, "Breakfast of Champions." Breakfast of Champions. Stupid. But Robbie really believed all that stuff about Joe Louis and Stan Musial eating it all the time.

"Sue," I said. "Do you want to come with me to bring Samantha home?"

"I can't," she said. "Miss Hurley asked me to be at the library by ten."

"How come?" I said. "You told me you didn't have to go in until Monday."

"Miss Hurley, that's how come," she said. "She wants the weekends off from now on, so I have to go in with the other librarian." Then, turning to my mother, she said, "You know, Mom, I wouldn't have taken this job if she had told me it would be every Saturday."

"Speak to her about it, Sue," my mother said. "I

think she should have told you before you took it."

I tapped the cereal box and said, "Are you coming with me, Rob? I've got the carriage all ready."

He pushed the box away slowly and gave me one of his looks. "What carriage?" When I told him, he jumped up and ran out to the front porch. I followed him.

"What do you think you're doing?" he said. "The dog can walk."

"Easy for you to say Samantha can walk. She's only a baby, and it's a long walk from Mr. Wood's house."

"The dog's not the one who's the baby," he said.

Susan walked by the door and Robbie called to her. "Sue, you've got to see what she's going to bring the dog home in."

She looked out the door and started to laugh, but then she stopped herself and said, "So what, Rob? You don't have to walk with her."

"Walk with her? I wouldn't be caught dead with her, but she's my sister and I'm not going to let anybody see her with this thing."

"I'm taking this carriage and I don't care what you say . . . you, you, you stupid ass."

My mother came out of the house; the screen door slammed behind her. "What kind of talk is that? I won't have that kind of talk around here. Apologize to him."

"But, Momma, he —"

"Don't 'Momma' me. Apologize to your brother."

"— but he's saying that because of Gloreen —"

"Amy, apologize. Now."

"— he acts like he's twenty-five when he's with —"

"AAAmy. Now."

"I'm sorry . . . but it's true. He acts like a big shot when he's around Gloreen. Well, he doesn't have to walk with me. Celie doesn't care if I take Samantha home in the carriage."

"I had no intention of walking with her, did I, Sue?"

"Keep me out of this," Sue said, walking back into the house.

My mother went over to Robbie and put her arm on his shoulder and said, "Rob, she can walk by herself. She's a big girl now."

"Only in size," he said.

"Did you hear what he said, Momma? How come he doesn't have to apologize?"

"That wasn't very nice, Rob," my mother said, shaking her head. She walked into the house, leaving Rob and me and the carriage.

"Stupid ass," I whispered, as I pushed the carriage. "Big old stupid ass."

When I got to the end of the driveway, I yelled, "Samantha is mine. All mine."

Robbie didn't answer me.

"Did you hear me? She's mine."

But Robbie had gone back inside.

I walked over to Celie's and sat down under her father's grape arbor to wait for her. It was cool under there, and I could see the beginnings of the grapes. I heard Celie calling good-bye to her mother as she left the house. She came up beside me and put her hand on the other side of the carriage, and the two of us took turns pushing it to Mr. Wood's.

It was kind of sad watching Samantha leave the box, knowing that she'd probably never see her mother again. She was the last one to leave. She licked my hand and she didn't mind when I picked her up and put her in the carriage. She curled up and her tail began to wag a little. I pulled the hood of the carriage up, said good-bye to Mr. Wood's sister, and then Celie and I started home. Samantha was asleep by the time we got to the 88's, and so Celie and I picked the carriage up, Celie holding the back while I held the handle. We struggled up the stairs like ants carrying a grasshopper, and when we got halfway up, Celie tripped and the carriage fell against me, knocking me down. I held the handle real tight, and when we got the carriage safely on the landing, we looked in. Samantha was still curled up, sleeping like a little baby.

When Samantha was finally in her bed beside my bed, I went out into the hall, picked up the telephone, and dialed my aunt's number.

"Aunt Emma," I said when I heard her voice, "tell Baron he's got a little sister and her name is Samantha. After Uncle Sam."

9

The telephone woke me up that Saturday morning. Usually I'm the first one to answer it, racing everybody to get to it. But that day, I was too tired. We'd worked all week on the doghouse, and it wasn't even finished. I still had a lot more sanding to do. Robbie kept leaving me to go to Gloreen's house.

I closed my eyes, turned over, and tried to go back to sleep, but I couldn't. When I had school, I never slept on Saturdays, but in the summer I sometimes did, because every day was Saturday. Except for Sunday, when I had to go to church.

The telephone kept ringing and I heard my father's footsteps coming down the hall. He picked up the telephone and said, "Good morning." He always says that when he answers the telephone in the morning. It sounds so silly. I always say, "Hello, who's this?" But he never does.

I could hear Samantha crying, so I got up and went over to her bed, but she was gone. Robbie got me so mad. Samantha was supposed to sleep with me, but every night since she'd been home, Robbie had sneaked in during the night and taken her into his room.

I started down the hall to Robbie's room, and when

I passed my father, I smiled and waved, but he didn't smile and wave back. He was so busy talking on the telephone he didn't even see me.

I banged on Robbie's door and put my head in and said, "Why'd you do it again? I told you not to take her."

"I didn't take him. I never take him," he said. Samantha was sleeping on the pillow next to Robbie's head. "Sam comes in to me. He had to pee. Maybe he'd stay in with you once in a while if you got up to take him out. What do you need, a bomb to wake you up?"

"You say that every time I find her in here."

"Well, it's the truth."

I picked up Samantha and brought her out into the backyard and let her run around. After a while, she began to sniff around, and when she was finished, I took her back into the house and got her breakfast.

I filled her water bowl and then put in a little milk. "Too much milk is bad for puppies," the vet had said. But she loved milk, and I always sneaked her some, just like we did for Baron.

I took down the Cheerios, and got a banana from the fruit basket and sat down and began to slice it. I love bananas. I love any kind of fruit. Whenever my father sees me eating an apple or an orange, he says, in a voice he calls his W. C. Fields voice, "Amy, my little chickadee, you'd better marry a fruit man."

I poured milk over the cereal and sprinkled sugar on top and began to eat. The Cheerios were little lifesavers swimming around in the milk, and when I got to the bottom of the bowl, I picked it up and let the cool, sweet milk fill my mouth and go down my throat.

The door to the kitchen swung open, and my father came in. He still had his pajaamas on, but he wasn't wearing his robe or slippers. His hair was standing up in back and it made him look funny. I said, "Hi, Daddy," and he sort of waved his hand at me, but he didn't say good morning.

He went over to the stove and turned on the heat under the coffee. Then he went to the sink, poured himself a glass of water, and began to drink it very slowly. When he was finished, he put the glass in the sink, turned on the faucet, and let the water run in and then over the sides of the glass. The house was silent. Nothing moved. Except the water.

"Daddy," I said, "do you want me to fix you some breakfast?"

"No thanks, Amy. I'll eat when your mother gets up." Then he turned to me and said, "Try to be quiet this morning. Let her sleep for a while. She was really exhausted last night, and Saturday is always a busy day."

He turned back to the window and looked out into the backyard. "You people are doing a good job on that house."

He smoothed down his hair, poured himself a cup of coffee, and walked out onto the back porch. He held the screen door so it would close quietly. I could see him walking toward the doghouse in his bare feet, sipping his coffee and looking around the yard as though he had never been there before.

I put the cereal away, picked Samantha up, and went out into the yard. "Daddy," I said, "are you feeling all right? You don't have your slippers on. You want me to get them for you?"

He shook his head and motioned for me to come over to him. I walked over, and when I got to him he put his arm around my shoulders and just stood drinking the coffee, not saying anything. After a while, we walked over to the lawn swing and sat down. I held Samantha in my lap and my father started to pump the swing with his feet. He started slow. Then a little faster. And then very fast until a breeze blew cool against our faces.

"Do you remember when we got this?" he asked.

I nodded my head.

He knew I remembered. I had had the chicken pox and he had driven to Sears, Roebuck in Boston and tied it to the top of the car and brought it home. My mother was working at the hospital all that summer, and Mrs. Breene and I sat in it every day until I was better. I pretended it was a ship and it was going to take Mrs. Breene and me to Florida to see Grandpa Amory. The awning was the sail and I was the captain. . . .

"I remember," I said.

He smiled and nodded. "Dr. Shermond said you were the last kid on the eastern seaboard to have chicken pox. Was it June or July?"

"It was July fourth," I said. "Remember Momma wouldn't let me go down to the beach to see the fireworks and you sneaked me some sparklers?"

He laughed a little. "That was Robbie's first year at camp," he said. "His first year, and he tied for best camper." He stopped smiling. Then he looked into his cup, swished the coffee around, and put it up to his lips, but he didn't drink it. He poured it onto the grass and it splattered onto his pajamas, but he didn't seem to care. Then he messed up my hair and said, "I'm going to get showered and wake Mom up. I told Susan I'd get her to the library by ten."

I kept pumping the swing and hugging Samantha. Then I remembered my mother had baked cookies last night and instead of raisins, she had put chocolate pieces in them. She was getting good about putting chocolate pieces in cookies. I jumped off the swing with Samantha and walked to the house, closing the screen door silently behind me. Then I got some cookies and started upstairs.

When I passed my mother's room, she was standing in the doorway, all dressed.

"Where are you going?" I asked.

"We're going to drop Susan at the library and then Daddy and I have to go into Boston for a little bit. We should be back around four."

"Is it okay if I go downtown with Celie after Robbie and I finish sanding the house?"

She looked at me and said, "Robbie is coming with us. Dr. Shermond called this morning. He wants to run another test on Rob."

"What kind of test? Robbie just went to Dr. Shermond's last week."

"One that has to be done in the city."

"What's he testing him for?"

"It's probably just a viral infection. But he wants to check Rob out before he leaves for camp."

"Are you sure?"

"Yes, I'm pretty sure."

"Is it okay if I go downtown with Celie?" I asked again.

"Check it out with Mrs. Breene."

"I guess I can forget it, then. The last time I asked her, she came with us and it took us two hours to walk back up the eighty-eights."

"Amy, please," my mother said in the voice she used when she was losing her patience.

"Well, it's true. She puffed all the way up."

Mrs. Breene could be a pain sometimes. But I loved her a lot. When I was little and my mother got stuck at the hospital, she'd meet me at school and walk me home. She almost never got mad and she made fudge and taught me how to crochet doll's clothes. My mother couldn't do stuff like that.

"Amy," Robbie yelled when I passed his room, "do some more sanding while I'm gone, and when I get back maybe I can start to put it together."

"I'll get Celie to help me. She's good at things like that," I said. "Couldn't we paint it yellow when it's finished?"

He was feeding his fish but he turned around and said, "Do you ever take no for an answer? Yellow is a dumb color. I told you I'm painting it blue. B-L-U-E. BLUE."

"How come everything has got to be what you say?"

"Because I'm building the house."

"Well, you'd never know it. You're always telling me how tired you are. Or you sneak off to Gloreen's, Robert. You sneak off to Gloreen's." And before he could say anything, I ran back to my room.

"Ellen," my father called, from downstairs. "We're back. Are you ready?"

After I saw Mrs. Breene and told her that Celie was coming to help me and she'd probably stay for lunch, I went out into the yard, got the roof out of the garage, and began sanding. I hated to admit it, but I was getting to like it. When I rubbed my hand over the wood that I had sanded, it felt warm and smooth. Like my mother's silk dress. When Celie came, she sanded one side of the roof and I did the other.

"Lunchtime," Mrs. Breene called out from the porch. The table was set for three. Mrs. Breene had cut the sandwiches into four pieces, the way she always did, and there was a big olive in the center of each one. She'd brought a little bag of potato chips and piled them on the side. My mother never bought potato chips, but she never told Mrs. Breene not to bring them.

We sat and ate the sandwiches and drank lemonade and talked. I got Mrs. Breene to tell us the story about the cemetery. She told all kinds of stories. But my favorite one was about the hands sticking up all over the cemetery. "Do you know whose arms are sticking up and why?" she'd ask. I always shook my head. And then she'd say, "Why, it's all those fresh children who answered back and sassed their mothers and fathers."

Susan never believed her. But Robbie and I did. I don't think Robbie believed it now, but I did, and every once in a while I'd nag my mother and father to take me to a cemetery where I could see for myself. But they always said no. I always thought that maybe, one day, Celie would go with me.

"Amy," Mrs. Breene said, as she began to clear the dishes, "I forgot to tell you I'm going to visit Raymond in Ohio. I'm leaving tomorrow on the one o'clock flight."

I was really surprised, because Mrs. Breene's husband was very stingy. He wouldn't even let her put the lights on in the kitchen on a dark day, and all the bulbs in the house were about twenty watts.

"Raymond sent us plane tickets," she said. "Jo just had another baby."

"Is Mr. Breene going with you?"

She shook her head. "Raymond sent him a ticket, but you know Mr. Breene. He told Raymond he was afraid of flying, so he cashed it in and put the money in the bank. I'll never understand that man, and I've been married to him for forty-two years."

She leaned over and wiped the crumbs from the table and said, "Do you know how much he got for the ticket?"

I shook my head.

"Thirty dollars and seventy-five cents."

She stood up, resting the hand holding the crumbs on her other hand, and said, "Raymond's no fool, you know. Do you know what he said to me, Amy?"

"No, what?" I asked.

" 'Mom,' he said, 'I'm sending one-way tickets because Pop will end up cashing his in. I'll send you back first class.' " And she started to laugh, and so did we.

When all the dishes had been cleared away, I picked up Samantha's bed very carefully. She was curled up in one corner, sound asleep. I brought her outside and put her under the tree so she could get some air, and Celie and I began to sand again.

We worked for a long time and when I went into the house to get some lemonade I heard Mrs. Breene on the telephone. "Don't you worry, Ellen, I'll just call Mr. Breene to tell him I'll be late. You have a real good dinner. It's not often you get a chance to have dinner in Boston."

I turned and ran back to Celie and said, "Boy, does that get me mad. They're in Boston. Robbie gets to have dinner in Boston and I get to have meatloaf with Mrs. Breene and Susan."

We started sanding again, and then I remembered Sam. I ran over to her bed, but she was gone. "Celie," I screamed as I ran into the house. "Look for her out here."

I looked in the kitchen and then in the living room and in my father's study and all over the first floor. Then I ran up the stairs as fast as I could and went into my room. The pillow that she used for a bed was empty. I raced through the hall and into Robbie's room. And there she was. All curled up like a little black furry ball, fast asleep on Robbie's pillow.

10

I really hated Dr. Shermond now, because just when it seemed as though everything was going back to the way it used to be, my mother told me that Robbie had to go to the hospital and Mrs. Van was coming. Mrs. Van was just about my most unfavorite person, and unless my mother changed her mind, she'd be here for lunch.

"Rob," I said, putting my head into his room, "did you know Mrs. Van's coming? Can you believe Momma would do that?"

He stuffed his comic books into his suitcase and sat on the lid to close it. "Now, now, m'dear, don't you get carried away," Robbie said, imitating her. "Mrs. Van'll fix you some nice lemonade with frozen butter cubes to cool it off. . . ."

"Easy for you to say. You won't have to listen to her," I said as I ran down the stairs and into the kitchen.

"Momma, please don't get Mrs. Van to stay," I said. "Susan and I can take care of the house. I promise, I'll be real good. I'll do anything Susan tells me to do. Only please don't get Mrs. Van. She stinks."

My father got up from his chair, closed the kitchen door, and leaned against it. "Amy," he said in a quiet voice, not bothering to turn around, "don't make things more difficult. Your mother is going to stay at Aunt Jane's so she can be close to the hospital."

"That's dumb," I said. "The tests won't take that long. Robbie'll be in the hospital only for a couple of days. Susan can take some days off and you can drive Momma to the hospital."

He turned and put his hand on my shoulder. "Amy, listen to me. Your brother is sick. He won't be home in a few days. Do you understand?"

"No," I said, "I don't."

Susan was sitting at the table, pushing her eggs around. I went over to her and said, "Susan, please tell Momma how terrible it is when Mrs. Van is here. Please."

She didn't answer. I pulled on her arm and said, "Susan, please."

She looked at me and said, "Amy, stop it. You're making things worse." She pushed her plate away and got up and walked outside.

My mother started to clear the table. She didn't say anything, but when she looked over at my father, she shook her head, the way she does when she's upset.

"Why can't you ask Mrs. Breene, Momma?" I said. "Mrs. Van can't even cook an egg."

"Mrs. Breene is in Ohio."

"Then ask Aunt Emma to come. . . ."

"She can't leave Uncle Sam in the condition he's in. His back isn't any better than when you saw him last week."

She reached out to me, but I pulled back. "Amy,

you haven't been listening to Daddy and me." She pushed her hair back with both hands, her palms over her ears, as though she didn't want to hear her own words. "Dr. Shermond said Robbie will be in the hospital for a while. A long while." And then, in a hoarse voice she said slowly, "Robbie's not going in for tests. He . . . he . . ." Then she stopped and turned to my father. He took her hand and put it up to his cheek.

"Amy," he said gently, "Robbie has leukemia."

"What's that?" I yelled. "What do you mean?"

"It means that Robbie is very sick. . . ."

"Momma said it was a virus. She said that —"

"That was at first," he said. "He's already had all the tests, and they show something more. . . ."

I ground my teeth back and forth and started to hum until I couldn't hear him anymore. Robbie couldn't be that sick. He couldn't. He was in his room, feeding his fish, just like he always did. When my father stopped talking, I turned away and walked over to the refrigerator. I took out some orange juice, poured it into a glass, and watched as it fell to the bottom, making bubbles as it splashed. One big bubble got stuck on the side of the glass.

"Amy, did you hear what Daddy said?" my mother asked.

I pushed my finger in the glass and broke the bubble.

That stupid old doctor. Robbie would show him. He'd be home *before* Sunday.

My mother walked over and turned me toward her. She looked right at me and in a voice barely above a whisper said, "Amy, I wish this weren't going on. I wish it more than anything, but sooner or later, you're going to have to accept the fact that your brother won't be home on Sunday. Mrs. Van may not be the best cook, but she's reliable. Daddy will be home most nights, so please don't make it more difficult than it is. Promise me, Amy. Promise?"

I nodded, then finished the juice, breaking even the littlest bubbles.

Why did Robbie have to go to the hospital? Why did Mrs. Van have to come with her big white shoes and that dumb white uniform, pretending she was a nurse or something? She wasn't anything but a big, fat, crabby old lady with skinny legs who never stopped talking, especially about Lee Howard. She listened to him on the radio every night, and then she'd tell us all about him the next morning. "Do you know what Lee had to say about television last night?" And then she'd answer herself, "Lee said it's a fad that won't last the year. I tell you, he's one smart fella." I hated Lee and I hated her. But she was coming and Robbie wouldn't be here. He wouldn't be here to do his imitations of her and make me laugh. I put my glass in the sink, then started toward the door.

"Amy," my father said, "I'm going to go over to pick up Mrs. Van. Why don't you come along?"

"No, thank you," I said. "I'd rather make friends with Roberta Barry than be in the car with Mrs. Van."

I picked up Samantha, pushed the screen door open, and went out to the yard. When I got to the clothesline, I walked through the clothes that my mother had hung to dry. Right through my father's shirts, and then through Robbie's pants, letting them slide across my face and over the top of my head and then drop down. I got on the swing and sat looking at the clothes. Robbie's pants were next to my shorts. I began to push the swing until it couldn't go any faster.

The summer was supposed to be the best time of the year, and it wasn't. Robbie was being a pain, too. He kept saying he was feeling tired. Every time we started to work on the doghouse, he'd say maybe he'd better read. Or he'd call Gloreen and go over to her house or she'd come over and they'd sit on the porch talking.

"What's the matter, Robert?" I'd say. "Are you in love with Gloreen? Are you in love with Gloreen?"

But Robbie said he didn't think I was funny and that if I didn't like it, I could lump it. And now he had to go into the hospital and my mother was going to stay in Boston and Mrs. Van was coming. It was a terrible summer. I could hardly wait for things to be the same. I could hardly wait for Robbie to be back home and for my mother to be here. And I could hardly wait for Mrs. Van to pack her bag and go home.

I got off the swing and held Samantha close to me, her breath warming my neck. I walked around to the sunny side of the house and sat down on the ground. I looked over at the doghouse and said, "Samantha, maybe I'll get Celie to help me finish. And then when Rob gets home, he can paint it. Or maybe I'll paint it and surprise him."

Everything seemed different. The grass needed to

be cut. My father mowed the grass every Saturday, but he hadn't done it this week. Maybe I'd do that and surprise him, too. Nothing was the same. My mother looked worried all the time and I heard her telling my father that he was going to make himself sick if he didn't take care of himself.

He wasn't cooking anymore, and he wasn't reading his books. He just walked back and forth around the house. Susan wasn't the same, either. She'd been staying at the library more and she didn't talk to Stanley on the telephone so long. And one night, I heard her crying.

I squeezed Samantha real tight. "You're the only person in this house who's the same. . . ."

"Amy," my father called. "Come on in. Mrs. Van would like to see you."

"Well, I don't want to see her," I said to Samantha. "Fat old turkey legs." I hugged Samantha again and walked back toward the house.

There she was, standing in the kitchen in her white uniform and big white shoes, holding her stupid purple and gold bag.

"Well, now, look at Miss Amy," she said. "She got taller and she seems to have thinned out a bit. Never thought that would happen."

Even our kitchen looked different with Mrs. Van standing in it. When my mother stood at the sink and the sun came through the window, it shone on her, and her shadow crossed over the floor and onto the table. But when Mrs. Van was in our kitchen, the sun never seemed to be there.

"Amy," my father said, "why don't you bring Mrs. Van's bag up to the guest room? Then maybe you can help her with lunch."

I didn't want to help her up with her bag. I didn't want any lunch she would make. Everything she made was greasy.

"Well, well," she'd say, "we're fresh out of butter. Better put that on top of the list today. Two pounds of butter."

I told her that my mother said butter was bad for you, but she said Lee Howard thought that was a lot of crazy talk. "Lee says butter is no worse for you than margarine. Why, he says margarine is just yellow lard. And he knows what he's talking about, dearie."

I dropped Mrs. Van's bag on the floor in the guest room and went to Robbie's room. He was putting the last bit of food in his fish tank.

"Want me to take care of your fish, Robbie?" I said. "I'll take real good care of them. I'll even sleep in here to keep them company."

Robbie kept staring at the fish tank. "Sure, Amy," he said, "but you don't have to sleep in here."

"Robbie," my father called, from the bottom of the stairs, "we're all ready."

"I'm coming," Robbie called. Then he turned to me and said, "Make sure you take good care of Sam while I'm gone."

"You can sleep with her for a week when you get home," I said. "I won't even argue."

But Robbie didn't answer me. He just picked up his bag and walked out of his room.

"Remember, Amy, when I get home, Sam gets to sleep with me," he called back over his shoulder.

"I just said that," I said.

Then I went into my bedroom and looked out the window until I saw them come out of the house. They walked down the path that led to the garage. The geraniums my mother always planted weren't there this summer. Everything looked so different. Even Robbie. His hands were pale and I could see his veins. But things would change when he came home. Everything would go back to the way it was. I ran from my bedroom, out the front door, and over to the car. Susan was giving Robbie a hug, and when she was finished, I grabbed him by the arm and said, "See you Sunday, Rob."

Then I put my arms around him and hugged him real hard and whispered, "See you Sunday."

My mother stood watching, and I could see tears starting in the corner of her eyes My father helped her into the car and said to Robbie in a real low voice, "Rob . . . it's time to go."

"Amy, be as helpful as you can to Mrs. Van," my mother called from the car. "Help her settle in. You too, Sue."

"Help her settle in?" I said. "She took over the whole house the last time." I put my head near the window and said to Robbie, "Remember when she told us the living room was hers from seven until eleven? 'Lee is on and I don't want any nonsense going on. He's my all-time favorite.' Remember, Rob?"

But Robbie didn't answer me.

My father started the car and when he began to back out of the driveway, I followed them, waving to Robbie. And when the car turned onto the street, I stood there waving my arm until I couldn't see the car anymore. I stood there for a long time, just looking at the empty street.

"Amy," Susan called. "Let's give Sam a bath."

I shook my head, but she said, "Come on, Amy. We're going to give Sam a bath."

I turned around and walked toward her, and when I got beside her, she put her arm around my shoulders and the two of us walked back into the house. "Want to come to the movies with Stanley and me tomorrow?" she asked.

I nodded my head, and she said, "I'll even pay your way."

11

The street lamp shone in my window and lit up the clock on my table. It was nine o'clock. Mrs. Van was laughing that crazy laugh of hers. It bounced from the living room and then up the stairs and into my room.

It was so hot in my room, I couldn't sleep. Robbie hadn't come home on Sunday, and sometimes when I was alone, I got scared. Especially when it got dark. I wished he weren't in the hospital. I wished he were home. Or even in camp.

I reached out and put my light on, picked up my book, and started to read, but I felt too hot, and so I picked Samantha up and crept downstairs. Mrs. Van was still laughing. ". . . Yessirree, all you folks out in Radioland, this here is your friend Lee, and I'll be with you . . ."

I tiptoed into the kitchen, took some fruit and some dog biscuits for Samantha, and closed the screen door quietly behind me. I got the flashlight my father always left by the back door and started toward the swing.

"Come on, Samantha," I said, "I'm going to read to you and we're going to have a picnic. You look hot, too."

Samantha had never even had a chance to cool off in her doghouse. Celie and I had sanded everything and Bootsy had helped us put it together, but it wasn't painted. Whenever I talked to Robbie on the phone, he kept saying he wanted to paint it himself when he got home.

"Don't paint it," he'd say. "I'm saving that job for myself."

Most of the time when we talked on the phone, I'd complain about Mrs. Van. One day he did an imitation of her: "Now, Amy, don't say you don't like my cooking. Doesn't everybody like butter on their bacon? Herman and Gladys do. And they just love it when I put a big fat lump in their coffee. Does a person good to have fat coffee."

But most of the time when I talked to Robbie, he'd just say a couple of things and then he'd give the telephone to my mother, and she didn't want to hear all my complaints about Mrs. Van. She kept saying, "Amy, it takes all kinds of people to make up this world, and Mrs. Van isn't the worst person you'll have to deal with."

"What does she know?" I said to Samantha. "She's never had to live with old fat butterball Mrs. Van Stupid, because if she did, she wouldn't ever have her in the house again. Isn't that right, Samantha?"

Samantha scratched her neck.

My father kind of knew what it was like. But he was home only in the morning and a little bit at night, because most times he'd have supper with my mother or he'd stop and do something at school. Last night when he got home, we picked Susan up at the library and then he stopped at Minnie's candy store and bought some ice cream. Even for Mrs. Van. But tonight he was staying at my aunt's. That made me so mad, because that meant that I'd be the only one Mrs. Van had to talk to in the morning. Susan usually slept late, and then she had to work.

I got on the swing and began to push back and forth. I bit into a peach and the juice ran down my chin. I started to wipe it away, but Samantha began to lick me. It tickled and her tongue was warm and it made me feel good. When she was finished, I gave her a biscuit and held her on my lap.

I turned the flashlight on and pointed it toward the house, making big circles with it. Around and around the light went. First the kitchen. Then the dining room. Then Robbie's room. The leaves on the willow tree were moving just a little, and their shadows made small dark figures on Robbie's window. They moved slowly. I slowed the swing down and kept in time with them. Then I moved the light and shone it on the clothesline. It was empty. Just clothespins sticking up. Some sticking down. Then I put the light on the very top of the house and looked at the chimney. It made me think of last Christmas. "Look," my father had shouted on Christmas morning, "Old Saint Nick left his boots in our fireplace."

I wished I still believed in Santa.

"I wish Robbie were here, Samantha," I whispered. "I wish he were here."

Then I opened my book. It was *Through the Looking*

Glass. My father had told me that everybody should read it at least twice. "Once for pleasure," he'd said, "once to learn." I'd just started it for the second time and already I was on page ninety.

I always skip around when I read. I read what I like best and then go back and read the boring stuff. When I get tired of reading the boring stuff, I skip around until I find what I like.

"Samantha," I said, "look at this. Who does Humpty Dumpty look like? Little skinny legs and a big fat head and double chins. Who? Mrs. Van, that's who. Only Humpty Dumpty is bald and he's smiling. But that's who he looks like. Mrs. Van." I shone the light on the page and held it up for Samantha to see. "See?" I said. "He looks just like her. Big and fat and clumsy. I wish she'd sit on a wall and have a big fall, and when all the king's horses and all the king's men couldn't put her together again, I'd sit back and laugh."

Samantha began to chew at the book and I put it down. "Do you want to play Guess What I'm Thinking?" I said.

I loved to play that game. Whenever we were all together, my father would say "Let's play Guess What I'm Thinking." Someone would think of something, and then everybody would ask questions to see if they could figure out what the someone was thinking. I always won, because whenever anybody got close to guessing what I was thinking, I changed what I was thinking.

"What am I thinking, Samantha?" I said.

Samantha put her head on my lap and closed her

eyes. "Come on, Samantha. What am I thinking? Well, I'm thinking about Aunt Emma's birthday party. My father made a toast and thanked her for being there when his mother died. And he thanked Uncle Sam, too. Momma cried. So did I. Then he asked my mother to dance and he kept kissing her hair and when the music stopped, he kissed her lips."

I got up from the swing and held Samantha in my arms and danced around. "This is the way they danced that night." I put Samantha's cheek next to mine and held her paw out and we danced on the cool grass. And when we finished, I kissed the top of Samantha's head.

After a while, I got back on the swing and pushed it.

"You never saw Daddy cook in his funny hat, Samantha. Just wait until Robbie comes home. He'll fix dinner again for us and he'll make Italian food and put on his cooking hat and say the blessing in Italian, just like they do at Celie's house. And Momma will laugh. And Robbie will call me a weirdo again."

Samantha began to snore a little and I began to get tired. I put my head down and held Sam close to my chest. I tried to keep my eyes open, but they kept closing. The swing kept rocking and rocking and rocking, slower and slower and slower. . . .

I woke up shivering and looked around me, not knowing where I was. I heard rain falling. Everything was black, and my back hurt and my arm ached. I felt Samantha's fur rubbing against me. I sat up slowly and then I remembered where I was. I felt around for the flashlight. Samantha licked my hand. "I wonder what time it is? Nobody even missed us." She licked my hand again.

I put the light on, tucked Samantha under my arm, and started back to the house. The light on the back porch was off, and when I tried the door, it was locked. I went around on the path by the side of the house; the light fell on the bricks and on the flowerbeds where my mother's geraniums used to be. My feet were cold and my nose was running.

My mother always came into my room before she went to bed. But tonight nobody missed me. Not even Susan. And then I remembered that tonight was Miss Hurley's retirement party. Maybe Susan wasn't home yet.

I walked up the front stairs and onto the porch. I tried to open the door, but the screen door was locked. From the living room window, I could see Mrs. Van sitting in my father's chair, and I could hear Lee talking away on the radio beside her. Her head hung down and her chest heaved up and down. Asleep. I pushed my face up to the screen and called to her, softly . . . then louder. And then, real loud, "Mrs. Van. Mrs. Van, let me in." She didn't move.

The wind changed and rain began to blow onto the porch; the bushes scratched the stairs, and in the distance, I could hear the whistle of a train. "Mrs. Van!" I shouted. "Please let me in." She still didn't move.

The train whistle got softer and softer and my voice got louder and louder. I pressed my face into the screen, and when my tongue touched it, the sour taste of it made me shiver. Samantha began to bark, and I shouted to Mrs. Van again. She lifted her head a little. "Mrs. Van, it's me, Amy. Let me in."

"Who's that? Who's there?"

"It's me. Amy."

She put her hands on the sides of the chair and tried to get up. She couldn't. Then she leaned forward and tried to push herself up. ". . . and for all you folks who are still with me out there in Radioland, your old friend Lee will be with you until eleven. So sit back, relax, and we'll have ourselves a ball."

She slumped back into the chair and then slowly turned toward the window. "What are you doing out there?"

"I couldn't sleep. It was too hot, so I went on the swing."

"Swinging on a swing in the middle of the night; well, ain't that cute."

"I must have fallen asleep," I said.

"I must have fallen asleep," she said. "Is that all you have to say for yourself?"

"Can you open the door?"

"Can I open the door? Sure, I can open the door, but I'm not going to open the door until Lee here is over." She turned away, settled herself back in the chair, and put the radio on louder. "I didn't put you out there, dearie. You put yourself out."

The curtains blew against the screen, and the wind held them there. I could smell my mother's smell on them. I squeezed Samantha to me and slowly slid down to the floor. She licked my face and then put her head in my lap and fell asleep.

And when Lee said, "Goodnight out there, my radio friends. Ain't we had fun? You be good now, and re-member God helps those who help themselves, so you help yourself to another big dose of your old friend Lee. Seven o'clock sharp tomorrow night. I'll be wait-ing for you," Mrs. Van opened the door.

I was too tired to talk. I walked into the house, up the stairs, and into my room. I fell into bed and pulled the covers around me. I wanted to cry, but I wouldn't let Mrs. Van see me do that. I could hear her coming up the stairs, mumbling something about the craziest damned house she'd ever been in. After a little while, the light from a car's headlights came through my front window, crawled up the wall to my ceiling, and stopped. I heard Susan call goodnight to someone and then the light went back across my ceiling and down to my window. Then it was gone.

I turned and looked out the other window. The moon wasn't there anymore. It was hidden behind a cloud somewhere and the sky was all black. I wanted to wish for something, but I couldn't find a star. Then I remembered something Mrs. Breene had told me. "Amy," she'd said, "you have an eyelash on your cheek." And she took the lash from my cheek, put it on my finger and said, "Now wish on it and blow it away." I wished for something and it came true.

I jumped out of bed, put on my light, and looked in the mirror. None of my eyelashes had fallen out, so I pulled at one until it came out. I put it on my finger, closed my eyes, and wished. I kept my eyes closed for a long time, thinking about my wish and praying it would come true. Then I opened my eyes and blew at my eyelash until it flew away.

I got back into bed, pulled Samantha close to me, and was just about to tell her what I wished for when I remembered that when you tell someone what you're wishing, it won't come true.

"Samantha," I said. "Do you think it makes a difference if the eyelash falls out or if it's pulled out?" I pulled the covers around me. "I don't think it makes any difference."

I gave Samantha a kiss, pulled her closer, shut my eyes, and went to sleep.

12

 "I'm going down to the village; will you come with me?" I whispered into the telephone.

"It's only seven-thirty," Celie said. "Where're you going so early?"

"I'll tell you when I see you."

"Okay," she said. "I'll be ready in ten minutes. I think my mother needs some stuff at the bakery."

I gave Samantha her breakfast, took a banana from the bowl, and wrote Mrs. Van a note.

Dear Mrs. Van —

I went for a walk with Samantha and I'll be back in a while. I had a banana for breakfast.

Amy

I put Samantha's leash on and walked out the back door. She sniffed around, and when she finally peed, I led her through the field and over to Celie's house. The grass was higher than Samantha and felt cool against my legs. When Samantha saw Celie's mother in her vegetable garden, she began to wag her tail.

"Good morning," Mrs. DiCarlo called.

She was on her knees weeding, her hair stuffed under a red bandanna, and even though it was early, the sweat glistened when she lifted her face to the sun.

"I'll be back with the bread before lunch, Ma."

Her mother waved, then wiped her face on her sleeve.

"Celie," her father called, "check to see that the bread is fresh. *Capisci?*"

"Yes, Pa," she said, "I understand."

We walked to the 88's and when we got there, Celie said, "You didn't tell me where you're going."

"To Mrs. Breene's to find out Raymond's telephone number, and then I'm going to call Mrs. Breene and beg her to come home. . . ."

"Are you crazy? Mrs. Breene lives way at the end of the beach. It'll take us two hours to walk there. Why didn't you call him?"

"I tried to," I said, "but I never get an answer."

"Maybe he went to Ohio and we'll walk all that way for nothing."

I shook my head and said, "He'll be home. You'll see. He wouldn't spend the money to go to Ohio. Don't you remember what Mrs. Breene told us?"

"Well, we'd better walk fast. I'll be in trouble if I don't have the bread home for lunch," she said and she took my arm and we ran to the bottom of the stairs.

"Morning, Amy. Morning, Celie," Miss Buxton called as we passed the bakeshop.

"Do you believe her, Celie?" I whispered. "She's got her back to us and she sees us."

"Good morning," we said and kept walking.

We walked through the village, and when we got to the entrance of the schoolyard, we walked in and took the shortcut to the street that led to the bridge. When we passed by the door that went to Miss Finnegan's classroom, Celie began to sing:

"Old Finnegan had a steamboat
The steamboat had a bell
The steamboat went to heaven
But Old Finnegan went to hell-o
Operator, please give me number nine
And if you disconnect me
I will chop off your behind the frigerator
There was a piece of glass
Old Finnegan sat upon it
And it went right up her . . . ask me no more
*   questions."*

I started to laugh and so did Celie. Then she put Samantha in between us and took my hands and we began to twirl around and around, keeping time to her singing. We went around and around until Sam became a blur and my head felt funny. "Stop it, Celie," I said. "Stop it; my stomach feels sick."

We slowed down, and when we finally stopped, she put her hand on my shoulder to steady me. When she did, Samantha began to growl and bark at her. She ran around Celie's legs until I picked her up and patted her and said, "No, Samantha. Celie's not hurting me. She wouldn't do that."

"It's okay, Sam," Celie said, "I wouldn't hurt Amy. Except if I'm late with the bread, then I'll kill Amy. And it won't be from twirling."

She grabbed me by the hand and we started to run across the street and over to the bridge. We ran until we got to the long walkway to the beach. The Breenes lived in a tiny house at the very end of the beach road, the part that was filled with wild rosebushes on the beach side and eelgrass by the creek. When the tide went out, the creek side really stunk.

"I don't know how Martha puts up with that house in the winter," my mother would say. "It's bad enough in summer. But winter? There's no heat, except for the fireplace."

Mrs. Breene said she didn't mind, but I knew she liked to come to our house whenever she could. She'd always take her sewing and sit in my father's chair. And once, when my mother was in Florida with my Grandpa Amory, and I had a high fever, she stayed in my room all night because I thought I saw someone at my window. She said it was from the fever, but she stayed. I almost didn't miss my mother. Well, almost.

We walked for a long time on the beach road. Every once in a while, Samantha would try to run in the water and I'd have to pick her up. "You can't drink that water. I'll get you some at Mr. Breene's house," I said.

"Do you think he'll give us some, too?" Celie asked. "The way Mrs. Breene talks about him, maybe he won't."

When we got to the path that led to the Breenes'

house, I could tell the tide was getting low. The path was narrow and rosebushes pricked my legs and caught Celie's skirt.

"Boy," Celie said, "isn't there an easier way to get in here?"

"Yeah," I said. "But you need a car. The front of the house is right off the main road."

"Who's there?" someone shouted. "Who's trespassing?"

I could see Mr. Breene standing on his porch. He had an old baseball cap on, pulled so far down it made his ears stick out. He looked all gray, except for his suspenders. They were red with blue stripes. Even his pipe was gray. He had it in his mouth, but there was no smoke coming from it. Mrs. Breene's cat, Mattie, was sitting on the porch railing. She started to hiss when she saw Samantha.

"This here is private property," Mr. Breene shouted as he bent over the porch railing. "Confounded people who make their way onto someone's property . . . you two make your way back to the public part. You hear me? This here is private property."

"It's Amy, Mr. Breene. Amy Martin. Don't you remember me?"

"Who?"

"Amy Martin. Mrs. Breene's friend. Can my friend and I come up on the porch?"

"You're here now."

"Could you put Mattie in the house so Samantha won't get scared, Mr. Breene?"

"Anything else you'd care me to do, missy?"

"Samantha is awfully thirsty and we are, too."

He straightened up, put his pipe down, grabbed Mattie by the neck, and started for the door. "Confounded kids. Don't give a hoot for someone's privacy," he said. "Take a drink from the back hose, and see that you don't leave it dripping," he said, pushing Mattie in the door.

"Thanks, Mr. Breene . . . and then can I talk to you?"

"Damn pain in the ass . . ."

We put the hose on and drank for a long time. I cupped my hands for Samantha, and after she drank, she peed in the bushes. Then Celie took her finger and made a little spray out of the water and held it up. We stood under it and lifted our faces up and let the cool water splash down. Samantha kept shaking her fur all over. It felt so good to be cool.

"What in hell are you doing with that water?" Mr. Breene shouted as he came into the backyard. "Water costs money."

He pulled the hose out of Celie's hand and shut the water off. "Now what are you here for?" he said.

"I need to get Raymond's telephone number in Ohio. I want to call Mrs. Breene."

"You're aiming to call all the way to Ohio to talk to my wife? Why don't you write? Stamps only cost three cents."

I shook my head. "I have to tell her something."

"Mail only takes two or three days."

"But I have to talk to her now. Today."

"Don't care how you waste money, do you? My water. Your pa's phone."

I shrugged. He turned and went into the house, and after a while came out with the number scribbled on a piece of newspaper. "When you talk to Martha, tell her it's time for her to get on home."

"Do you miss her?" I said.

He shook his head a little and said, "My pants need fixing and the tomatoes need preserving. And that damned cat of hers is in heat."

I thanked him for the number, and Celie and I said good-bye and started back down the path.

"Hey, missy," he called. "Don't you tell her about my pants and the tomatoes. Just tell her it's time for her to come home."

"Want me to tell her about Mattie?"

He shrugged his shoulders and walked back up the porch steps, put his pipe back in his mouth, and sat down in Mrs. Breene's old rocking chair.

I had to carry Samantha because she kept getting stuck on the bushes. Celie pulled her skirt close to her and I tried to keep my legs away from the bushes, but every once in a while they'd brush against my legs, leaving tiny pink lines.

"Let's walk fast," Celie said. "I've got to get to the bakery and get the bread home before lunch."

"That's fine with me, because as soon as I get home, I'm going to call Mrs. Breene and beg her to come back." I breathed in until my chest hurt, squeezed Samantha, and whispered, "Part of my wish is *already* coming true."

13

The tide was coming back in and the breeze was getting cooler. When we got to the beach, we took our shoes off and went down to where the sand was just a little wet so we could go faster. Samantha ran ahead, kicking up little bits of sand with her paws. It felt so good to have my feet in the damp sand, but it made me sad, too. I thought of Robbie and all the other summers. The fun ones when we'd go clamming with my father. And last summer when my father and Robbie tried to teach me how to sail.

"Celie," I said, "remember when I told you Robbie tipped the sailboat and knocked my father down with the sail? It wasn't Rob. It was me."

"I knew that. What made you think of that now?"

"The ocean. Who told you it was me?"

"Nobody."

"How'd you know?" I said.

"Because when you get really mad or tell something that isn't true, you get red."

"I do not."

"You do, too."

"Give me a for-instance."

"Like the time you told your mother that you were coming to my house and you were really going downtown to meet Bootsy at Nino's."

"I never did that."

"You did so."

"Well, I don't remember."

We kept walking, and when we got to the end of the beach, we climbed back up to the walkway and put our shoes on. We were thirsty again, so we walked over to the water fountain at the end of the bridge. There were some kids waiting to get a drink. As soon as we got in line, I heard someone say, "Well, if it isn't Miss Fatty and Miss Pastafazool and their pet skunk."

I turned around. Peter and Roberta were sitting on the bench beside the fountain.

"What did you say?"

"You heard me," Roberta said.

"Take it back," I said, "or you're going to be sorry."

"Still talking like a big shot. Where's Bootsy and Patrick?"

"And where's your dumb monitor's belt?"

Celie turned around and said, "Don't bother answering her. She's a jerk."

"Didn't you hear what she said? She called you Miss Pastafazool. Don't you know what that means?"

"I heard her, but it doesn't matter. She's a dumb jerk. Forget it. Let's get a drink and get to the bakery." Then Celie looked at Roberta and said, "Cut it out, Roberta."

"Yeah," I said, "you'd better watch yourself."

"Says who?"

"Amy, don't listen to her," Celie said.

"But she called us —"

"Forget it," Celie said, and she turned the fountain on and took a long drink. When she was finished, she held the button down for me. I took a long drink, then I cupped my hands and bent down to give Samantha a drink. When I did, I felt something cold on my back.

I stood up and water poured down my shirt and into my shorts. I turned around. Roberta was standing with her arms folded and her eyes looking up like she didn't know what was going on. Peter was standing beside her. "Look at that, Peter," Roberta said. "Some people can't even take a drink of water without making a mess."

"You creeps," I yelled. "Look what you did to my shorts." I gave Roberta a push and then another one until she fell back onto the grass.

Samantha growled and started to run around Roberta, but Celie pulled her back.

"There," I said. "That's the push you said I gave you in the schoolyard, only now you don't have Miss Finnegan to come running and say, 'Oh my, dear, precious Roberta, that Amy is such a wicked girl. . . .'" Then I got on top of Roberta. "Now take back what you said, or I'll never get up. I'll sit on you until you're dead. Take it back," I screamed.

Peter tried to pull me off Roberta, but he couldn't because when I get mad, I get really strong. I could hear Celie calling to me and Samantha growling, but I kept yelling, "Take it back. Take it back."

"Okay. Okay," she said, "I take it back. Now get off me."

"Tell Celie you take it back."

". . . I take it back."

"And tell Samantha you take it back."

"I take it back. Get off me. I can't breathe."

I got up and backed away from her, wiping my face on my sleeve.

Roberta got up and walked over to where Peter was standing. She brushed herself off and then looked over at me and said in a real quiet voice, "How's your brother?"

I didn't answer her.

She turned to Peter and said, "Tell her what your mother heard, Peter. Tell her."

"Shut up, Roberta," Celie said. "Shut up." Then she pulled me by the arm and said, "Amy, let's go. Let's get to the bakeshop. Don't listen to her. She doesn't know what she's talking about."

I pushed Celie's arm away.

"Tell her, Peter."

Peter just stood there. And then Roberta said, "Okay, I'll tell her myself. Peter's mother said your brother's never getting out of that hospital. She said he's going to die there."

I stood there, shaking my head, looking at her. Just looking at her. I wanted to kill her. I wanted to get a big stick and hit her on the head until she was dead, but I couldn't move from where I was standing. I started to shiver.

"Liar," I said, in a voice that sounded like chalk squeaking on a blackboard. "Liar. Dirty, filthy liar."

"Come on, Amy," Celie said, "let's go."

"Liar," I screamed. "Stinking, rotten liar. Kids don't die. Only in accidents. You hear me? Kids don't die."

Celie grabbed me by the wrist, took Samantha by the leash, and pulled us toward home. And all the way home, I felt like my body was somebody else's. I couldn't talk. I couldn't cry. I couldn't feel.

"And where have you been?" I heard Mrs. Van say as I walked through the back door with Samantha. "You said you'd be back in a little while. Your mother called. . . ."

"I took a long walk with Samantha. And now I want to go to sleep."

"Well, you'd better give your mother a call. She wants to talk to you."

I walked through the kitchen, up the stairs, and into my mother and father's bedroom. I pulled down the spread, got into their bed, and picked up the telephone.

"Operator," I said, "I'd like to make a long distance call to Ohio. Mansfield, Ohio. I want to talk to my friend, Mrs. Breene."

14

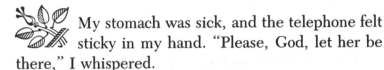My stomach was sick, and the telephone felt sticky in my hand. "Please, God, let her be there," I whispered.

"That number doesn't answer," the operator said.

"Please, operator," I said, "please keep ringing."

There was static on the telephone and then someone picked up the receiver and said, "Hello — who's using the phone?"

"Mrs. Breene, is that you?"

"Mrs. Who? . . ."

"I'm sorry, young lady," the operator said, "there's no answer at that number. I'll try it again and call you back. . . ."

"What number? Who is this?" And then I realized the voice was Mrs. Van's. I pressed the button down and put the receiver back in its place.

Mrs. Van's voice boomed all the way from the kitchen. "What in God's name do you think you're doing up there?"

I didn't answer her but rolled over to my father's side of the bed and put my face into Samantha's fur. And waited. Maybe the operator would call me back.

But maybe she wouldn't. Maybe Mrs. Breene wouldn't come. Maybe my mother would be really mad at me for calling her. Maybe Robbie wouldn't . . . I squeezed Sam's fur in my hands. She squealed and tried to pull away. "I'm sorry," I said, patting her head. "I'm really sorry. I'd never hurt you. Never."

The telephone rang, and I leaped across the bed and picked up the receiver.

"I've got it, Mrs. Van," I screamed. "Hello? I want to speak to Mrs. Breene."

"This is Mrs. Breene. Amy? Why, Amy, is that you?"

And when I heard her voice, I fell back on the pillow and said, "Mrs. Breene, please come home. Please. Mattie's in heat and Mr. Breene misses you and . . . and . . . Robbie's still in the hospital and Mrs. Van locked me out . . ."

The door opened and Mrs. Van filled the doorway. "Is that your mother you're carrying on with?" she said.

I put my hand over the receiver and nodded my head.

"Well, you tell her I want to speak to her. Don't you put that phone down until I've had my say." She started over toward the bed, pointing her finger at me, muttering, "Do I make myself clear?" Then she tapped her finger hard on my shoulder and when she did, Samantha jumped off the bed and began to bark and run around her, pulling at her stockings.

She backed away, shouting, "Damn pest of a dog. Look what he did to my stockings." She glared at me and said, "Don't you hang up that phone until I've had my say." Then she turned and stormed out of the room.

My hand slid from the receiver. My mouth was dry and my heart was pounding. I opened my mouth slowly and said, "Mrs. Breene, please. Please come home. I need you to be here."

Mrs. Van had her bag packed in two minutes when she heard Mrs. Breene was on her way home. "That lady must have nerves of steel to put up with this crowd," she said to my father as we got ready to go pick up Mrs. Breene at the airport.

My father didn't answer her. He took her suitcase and put it by the telephone where Mrs. Van stood calling her son. "That you, Gladys?" she said. "You get Herman right on over here. What's that? Well, I'll get him straightened out when I get there. Gladys? Gladys . . .?" She put the receiver down and said, "Must have been disconnected." She dialed again and after a while, she said, "Must be trouble on the line. Better call me a cab."

My father didn't answer but dialed the number for the cab, said good-bye to Mrs. Van, and told her to lock the door behind her and to leave the key under the mat. "You won't be needing it anymore," he said. Then he motioned for Susan and me to go out to the car and closed the door behind him.

Mrs. Breene's plane was late, and even though my father seemed nervous, he asked if we'd like to play Guess What I'm Thinking. But it wasn't much fun.

Susan didn't want to play and my father kept leaving to call my mother at the hospital. Then he'd pace up and down. Like the morning Dr. Shermond called. Only worse.

The plane finally came in, and he ran down to the gate. Susan followed him. When Mrs. Breene got off the plane, she hugged Susan and then turned to my father and put her arms around him. She held him like he was a little boy and then she began to rock back and forth, like my mother did when we were upset. I stood very still and watched. After a little while, he pulled away from her and she took his face in her hands and kissed him. I waited for a long minute and then raced down the ramp and across to the gate and threw myself at Mrs. Breene.

"Oh, my, it's good to see you, Amy," she said, opening up her arms and taking me in. "You almost knocked me down."

I stood and hugged her, feeling the warmth of her arms across my back, smelling her, thanking her for coming over and over again, and when my father told us it was time to go, I kissed her quickly and told my father I'd help him with her luggage.

"I should go away more often," Mrs. Breene said. "Why, this is the best reception I've ever had."

"And we're going out to supper, too," I said.

"No, no, no," she said, "I'll fix supper. I haven't made supper since I left home." And then, turning to my father, she said, "You just drop us off at home, Bob. Ellen needs you to be with her."

I didn't care about going out to eat now that she was here. Things would be different. Maybe Rob *would* come home this Sunday.

I bent over, picked up her biggest bag in my two hands, leaned back to balance myself, and staggered out to the car. I could have carried Mrs. Breene, too. Susan slipped her arm around her waist, and when we got to the car, my father helped Mrs. Breene into the front seat. Every time I looked at the back of her head, I felt better and better.

Susan drove in to the hospital with my father, and Mrs. Breene let me invite Celie to supper. The meat-loaf she made tasted like Toll House cookies with a hundred chocolate pieces in every one, and when it was time to clean up, she didn't even have to ask me to help.

"I can't believe Pa said I could stay overnight," Celie said, as we walked up the stairs and into her house. "I better get my things together fast before he changes his mind."

I could hardly believe it, too. Mr. DiCarlo never let Celie stay over at anybody's house. "You sleep in your own bed, in your own house," he'd say whenever Celie asked to stay over. "*Capisci?*"

I sat in the kitchen with her mother while Celie got her pajamas and toothbrush, and after a little while, Mrs. DiCarlo got up from her rocking chair and walked over to the pantry. She took out a cookie tin and put it on the table.

"Amy," she said, "take these home for your momma;

your poppa can take them into the hospital. A cup of tea and an anise cookie is good." Then she opened the box and took a cookie out and handed it to me. "You have one now."

I took a little bite and began to chew. I hated anise cookies, but Mrs. DiCarlo had baked them and I didn't want to hurt her feelings. When Celie's voice came from the hallway and her mother turned, I stuffed the cookie into my pocket.

"I'm ready," Celie said. "Let's go."

She called goodnight to her father and kissed her mother, and we walked out of the kitchen, down the stairs, and over to the field. I held my father's flashlight in one hand and the tin of cookies in the other. The field was dark and scary, because the street lamp wasn't bright enough to light the field. I kept waving the flashlight around, looking behind bushes and up into trees. "You think anyone was ever murdered in here?" I said.

"You're crazy, Amy. People don't get murdered in Manuet," she said. "Wait a minute. I take that back. My father almost murdered me yesterday when I didn't bring the bread home in time for lunch."

I started to laugh, but Celie said, "I'm serious. He was real mad." And then she swung her shopping bag around, knocking fireflies back into the darkness.

"I'm sorry," I said. Then I grabbed Celie's hand and pulled her across the field toward my house. We ran until we got to the back porch, and when we opened the kitchen door, Mrs. Breene was sitting at the table reading the paper, just the way she always did.

She looked up from the paper and smiled. "Well, that didn't take long. Got everything you need, Celie?"

Celie nodded.

"Look at this picture, girls," she said, pointing to a picture of a roof with a big television aerial on it. "Did you ever see anything like this? Why, it says here there are people who put up those aerials even if they don't have a TV. Seems they want to fool people into thinking they have one. Isn't that something?" And she began to laugh.

I looked at Celie and she shrugged. "It's terrible," I said.

I put the tin of cookies on the table and said, "Come on, Celie, I've got to feed Robbie's fish."

Lately I've been hating to go into Robbie's room. It doesn't smell like his room anymore. It smells like clean sheets all the time. And there's nothing on top of the bed but the spread. And it's not wrinkled. Robbie's comic books are all neat on his shelf and his drawers are shut tight; nothing hangs out anymore. "Robbie," my mother used to say, "don't you know how to close drawers?"

I walked over to the fish tank, opened the box of fish food, and measured out the amount Robbie had told me to give them.

"Celie," I said, "see that blue fish? Robbie's going to die when he comes home and sees how many babies she had. Twelve babies. More than Samantha's mother."

Celie put her face up to the glass and looked inside.

"How come fish can have twelve babies and dogs can have six and mothers usually only have one?"

I sprinkled the food into the tank and Celie put her hand in the water and swished it around. The fish began to swim around and kept coming up to nibble the food until it was all gone.

"I once saw a picture of a mother who had five babies," I said.

"Five babies? Are you serious?"

"I swear. I saw them in one of my father's old magazines."

Then I looked into the tank and said in a real quiet voice, "They'll probably never be lonely."

I brushed my hands over the fish tank, and the last bit of food fell on top of the water. The blue fish swam up and took every last piece. "Come on," I said, "let's go down and get something to eat. I'm starved."

The milk tasted better with Mrs. Breene here, and the cookies weren't all greasy, and the kitchen looked almost the same as when my mother was home. When we were finished, I cleared the table and put the milk away, and even though it was dark outside, I asked Mrs. Breene if we could take Samantha for a walk. "I promise we'll be back in ten minutes."

"No more than ten minutes," she said. "Take the flashlight and don't leave the block."

Samantha sniffed around the yard for a while and after she peed, she ran over to the doghouse and began to sniff again.

"She's probably sniffing for Rob," I said.

The air was cool and the wind was blowing just a little. The leaves from the willow tree brushed against the roof of the doghouse, making a sound like somebody whispering. We stood very, very still and listened.

"Robbie's going to paint it blue," I said.

"I know," Celie said.

Then Samantha began to bark and yank on her leash. She pulled me down the driveway and up the block with Celie running after us. When we got to the end, I could see a tiny light on Miss Swords's porch. Her house was always dark, even when the sun was shining.

I turned the flashlight on and shined it at her porch. She was sitting in her rocking chair with Sweet Sally on her lap. "Who's there?" she called.

I aimed the light down, and in the dark we could hear the porch creak as she rocked back and forth. We stood still. "I want to know who's there."

Celie took the flashlight out of my hand and put it under her chin so that it lit up part of her chin and the tip of her nose and a spot on her forehead. Then she said in a low, low voice, "The Shadow knows . . . the Shadow knows. . . ."

But when I heard the rocker bang against the railing, and Sweet Sally's paws running from the porch, I picked Samantha up and we ran down the block as fast as we could and into the backyard. When I got my breath, I said, "Do you think she knew who it was?"

"What's the difference?" Celie said. "She'll blame us anyway. . . . 'Mizz Martin, that child of yours is up to no good. If she were my child, I'd send her to boarding school. In Australia.' "

"How come you said Australia? That's where Mrs. Van says Herman wants to go to live." And then I stuck my stomach way out and put my chin on my chest and said, "Come on, there, dearie, it's time for Lee. Don't you know, he's just about the smartest young fella to come to these parts in a long time. And he likes butter. Real butter. Not that margarine crap that Mizz Martin here uses."

"How many pounds of butter did she use?"

"Forty-two," I said. And then Celie and I ran back to the house, kissed Mrs. Breene goodnight, and went up to my room and got undressed.

"Put 'Your Ten Top Tunes' on," Celie said. "Jemma told me Stubby Jones is going to sing the number one song tonight."

"Stubby. Is that a stupid name or is that a stupid name?" I said, and I started to laugh. Then I remembered how Robbie used to tease Susan when she listened to Stubby Jones and I stopped laughing and climbed into bed. Celie got in beside me.

"I wish Rob were here to tease us."

Celie didn't say anything.

"I miss him, Celie; I want him to come home. Do you miss him?"

She didn't answer. She turned her back to me and pulled the covers around her.

"You're taking all the covers," I said.

"I'm sorry," she said and pushed some over to me. "Goodnight, Amy."

"I'm not going to sleep. Are you?"

"Mmnnnnn."

I turned toward the window and looked out. The moon looked like a banana. A faraway banana. "Did you know that some part of the same moon shines somewhere every single night?" I said. "It's true. Robbie told me."

Celie didn't answer me.

"Are you sleeping?"

"No."

"How come you're so quiet? You said you wanted to listen to Stubby. You okay?"

"I'm okay."

"You sure?"

"I'm sure." And then she said very slowly, "Amy, my mother told me Robbie isn't ever coming home. She said he's too sick to come home."

"What?"

Celie didn't answer.

I sat up. "What did you say?"

She still didn't answer.

I knelt beside her and pushed her on her back. "What did you say?" I screamed. "What did you say?"

Celie looked up at me and in a voice barely above a whisper said, "I said my mother said Robbie is too sick to come home."

"Nobody says that," I yelled. "Nobody. He *is* coming home. He *is* coming home. Do you hear me? He *is*. He *is*."

Celie reached out to me and put her hand on my arm. "Amy," she said softly, "remember when Bootsy's cat got run over? Do you remember how you almost made Bootsy believe she wasn't dead because you said cats have nine lives . . . ?"

"Shut up."

She tried to put her hand on my shoulder. "Don't you touch me," I said, punching her arm away. "Don't you ever touch me again."

Celie's eyes got watery. "Amy," she said, "sometimes you only believe what you want to. . . ."

"Shut up. You shut up," I screamed. "I don't have to listen to you." My chest moved up and down. "Get out!"

"Amy, I'm sorry. . . ."

"He *is* coming home. He *is* coming home. You'll see."

Then I jumped out of bed, grabbed the cookie Celie's mother had given me, crumbled it into a million pieces, and threw them at her. "I hate your mother. And I hate her cookies."

Mrs. Breene burst into my room. "Amy, what is it? What is it? What's gotten into you?"

But I didn't answer her. I ran down the stairs, screaming back at Celie, "Get out of here! Get out of here and don't come back." I flung the kitchen door open and picked up the tin of cookies. I threw the cookies on the floor and stamped on them until they were nothing but a pile of crumbs.

"Amy. Amy," I could hear Mrs. Breene call, as she came down the stairs, "Celie didn't mean . . ."

And when Celie and Mrs. Breene came into the kitchen, I grabbed Celie's arm and pushed her across the room and out the screen door. Even Mrs. Breene couldn't stop me. I threw the cookie tin after her and shouted, "That's what I think of your mother and her cookies."

Mrs. Breene tried to hold me. "Oh, Amy," she said, "she was trying to help you." I pushed her away and ran up to my room and fell into bed. I put the radio on real loud and pulled the covers over my head. "Don't cry," I said into my pillow. "Don't you dare cry." Then I closed my eyes and didn't open them until the first light from the sun shone on them.

15

Sometimes I wondered about Mrs. Breene. Like last night. She took Celie's side. I wish she'd go home, too. I want just my family to be here.

"Amy," Mrs. Breene called, "I've got breakfast on the table."

She can just keep it there. I don't care what she tells my father when he comes home. If I want to stay in my room all day and sulk, that's just what I'm going to do. I pulled the covers over my head when I heard her coming up the stairs. "Amy," she called, "come on now. Your breakfast will get cold."

She came into my room and took a deep breath. The stairs really made her puff. "Are you really sleeping, or are you just pretending?"

I didn't answer. My head hurt, and it was so hot and sticky under the covers I couldn't breathe. After a while I had to answer.

"I don't feel like eating," I said. "I'll eat later."

"It's your favorite. French toast. And I told Celie she could come on over."

I threw the covers off and stood up in bed. "I don't want her for breakfast, or lunch, or supper, or sleeping in this house. I don't want her anywhere near me.

She's a dumb friend and I never want to see her again."

Mrs. Breene looked over at me and smoothed her apron. I threw myself down on my bed, pulled the covers up, and closed my eyes. "You just tell Celie she can find herself another friend."

I could hear Mrs. Breene's stockings rubbing together, and I knew she was coming over to me. I pushed myself to the other side of the bed. "Celie doesn't want another friend," she said.

"Well, she doesn't have me anymore. She's a liar," I said. "What does her stupid mother know? I hate liars. I want to go back to sleep."

Mrs. Breene fixed the covers and smoothed my hair. "Do you want me to send Sam on up?" And when I didn't answer, she made her way out of my room, down the hall, and back downstairs. I could hear the swoosh of her stockings getting softer and softer.

How could Celie tell me that Robbie wasn't going to come home? What does her mother know, with her dumb old cookies? And Mrs. Breene, what does she know? Robbie *was* going to come home. He told me he would. "Samantha?" I said when I heard her coming up the stairs. "Come in here. Come on in to Amy."

I must have fallen asleep, because when I opened my eyes, the sun wasn't shining through my windows anymore. Samantha was still beside me. I put my arm around her and she began to lick my face. "Good old girl," I said. "You'll see. Robbie will be home soon. right, Sam?"

She just kept licking my face.

I got out of bed and went into the bathroom. Even there it looked different. Robbie's toothbrush still wasn't there and neither were his comic books. I washed my face and hands and brushed my hair and was just about to go downstairs when I heard Celie's voice.

"Amy," Mrs. Breene called. "Celie's down here. How about something to eat? It's almost two o'clock."

"I wouldn't eat with her if my life depended on it," I yelled down. "Tell her to go home."

I could hear some commotion downstairs, and then the screen door slammed. I ran into Robbie's room, where I could see the backyard, and saw Celie walk slowly back to her house.

"Serves you right," I said. But she couldn't hear me.

After I fed Robbie's fish I sat at his desk for a while and then decided to take Samantha for a walk. Just as I was about to go downstairs, the telephone rang.

"I've got it, Mrs. Breene," I called.

"Hello," I said.

"Amy, it's me. Robbie."

"Robbie! Hi. It's me, Amy. How do you feel?"

"All right. Did Dad call you?"

"No," I said. "He called Mrs. Breene from Aunt Jane's and told her Momma looked so tired he was going to stay with her to make sure she rested. Then he's going to take Susan home."

"They left here about fifteen minutes ago," Robbie said. "You sure he's going to stay in for a while?"

"Sure, I'm sure. He said he'd probably get home about nine o'clock."

"Is anyone listening on the extension?" Robbie asked.

"There's no one here except Mrs. Breene and Samantha and me."

"Make sure, will you?" he said.

I put the telephone down and went down the stairs very softly to make sure Mrs. Breene wasn't listening. She usually didn't, but I wanted to make sure. She was sitting in the kitchen, peeling carrots and listening to the radio.

"It's okay," I said.

"Listen to me. You've got to bring Sam here. I really need to see him. And you, too, Ame."

"What are you talking about, Robbie? You just saw her a few weeks ago. You'll be home soon. I'm taking good care of her and you should see your fish — one had some more babies. . . ."

"Amy, I've got to see Sam. Don't you understand? I've got to see him."

"How am I going to get Samantha into Boston? Can you tell me that?"

"I've been thinking you and Celie could take the train in this afternoon. I checked the schedule and there's one leaving at three-thirty. It'll get you to North Station at four. You could be here by four-thirty and home before dark."

Robbie's voice sounded funny and he kept taking deep breaths. I began to get scared. How could I get Samantha into Boston alone?

"Robbie," I said, "Celie and I had a big fight and I'm not speaking to her. Couldn't you wait till you get home to see her? Besides, I'm not old enough. They won't let me into the hospital."

"Thanks a lot, Amy. Thanks a lot," Robbie said. "Sometimes you really get me mad. I'd do it for you. You know I would."

I knew he would. And I knew I had to.

"Okay," I said. "But I only have seventy-five cents and I don't know how to get there."

"Take some of my paper route money. It's in my drawer," he said. "And when you get here, don't come in the main entrance and don't go up the stairs in the front. Go around to the delivery door — it leads right up to my room."

"What if it's locked?"

"It won't be," he said. "Remember, no main entrance and no front stairs — they don't go anywhere."

"What are they there for?"

"How should I know? They're just an old set of stairs. Forget them, Ame. Just do what I tell you."

"Okay, Rob." I said. "Maybe Sam can sleep with you for the night."

"No," he said, taking another deep breath, "I just want to see him again. Get a pencil. I'll give you directions."

I changed my clothes and took the afghan from my bed. Then I went into Robbie's room and took his brand-new camp duffel bag from the shelf and stuffed the afghan into it. I took three dollars from his drawer and whistled for Samantha.

"Come on," I said, "we've got a long way to go."

Mrs. Breene was still sitting at the kitchen table slicing carrots.

"I'm going to take Samantha for a long walk," I said. "Then maybe I'll go over to Celie's and make up with her. I'll probably have supper there, because Mrs. DiCarlo invited me before we had the fight."

My stomach felt sick and my face felt hot. Mrs. Breene turned to me and smiled and said, "That's more like my Amy. Celie didn't mean to hurt you. She was only trying . . ."

I turned away from her and went out the door.

"You call me from Celie's if you're going to be late," she called after me.

It was about three o'clock. I had a half hour to walk to the station and buy my ticket. I was scared. I wished somebody was with me. I pulled Samantha along because every time we passed a tree, she'd want to smell it and stop to pee. When I got to the top of the 88's, I stooped to pick her up and just as I did, I heard someone call my name.

It was Celie.

"Amy, wait," she called. "Wait for me."

When she caught up, she was out of breath, so we just stood for a while, looking at each other.

"Robbie called me from the hospital," she said. "I'm sorry, Amy. I'm really sorry if I upset you. I've got two dollars, and my mother made us sandwiches. I told her we were going to go to the park to roller-skate. I figured she wouldn't worry, and by the time she does, I can call and tell her I'm on my way."

I didn't answer. I pushed Sam toward her and she reached out and took her. We ran down the 88's and over to the station.

"Aren't you girls kind of young to be traveling into Boston alone?" the stationmaster said when we got up to the ticket window.

"I'm fourteen and my friend is thirteen," Celie said, crossing her fingers behind her. "Besides, my sister is getting on the train in Seaview. She told us to sit in the second car and she'd meet us there."

"Glad to hear that. The city's no place for little girls to be roaming around." He handed us our tickets and said, "I'm giving you half-fare seats, seeing as your sister is meeting you on board."

We put Sam in the duffel bag with the afghan wrapped around her. "Be good," I said. "I've got biscuits for you if you're good."

"Better give him one now," Celie said. "The train is coming in."

"Samantha," I whispered, "please, please be good. Don't bark. Please don't bark."

16

Celie and I sat down and waited for the train to start. My heart was pounding and my legs were shaking. "What if the conductor sees her?"

"Just keep the bag covered with the blanket," Celie said.

I could see the conductor start up the aisle. He didn't talk to anybody and he looked real grouchy. He just put his hand out, took the ticket, punched it, and gave it back. He didn't smile once, and when he started over to Celie and me, I really felt sick to my stomach.

Samantha started to cry a little, the way she does when she's scared. When I put my hand into the bag and patted her, she licked my hand. "Just one more minute," I whispered. I looked over at Celie. "What if he hears her?"

"It's too late to worry now. Here he comes."

The conductor walked over and held out his hand, and when Celie gave him our tickets he said, "Who are you kids traveling with? You've got half-fare seats here. You're supposed to have an adult with you on a half-fare seat."

I held my breath as the conductor looked at Celie, waiting for her to answer.

"You hear what I said?"

Celie looked up and said in a real serious voice, "My sister is meeting us at North Station."

"That doesn't entitle you to half-fare. The adult's got to be on the train with you."

"Oh, I know that," Celie said. "I meant she's meeting us in North Station because she smokes and my friend can't sit in the smoking car. She's got asthma." Celie poked me and I began to cough a little and then Samantha began to whimper more.

He looked over toward me and said, "What's that?"

I started to breathe hard and made a funny noise come from my throat. I sounded like I was having an attack.

"See?" Celie said. "She gets real bad sometimes."

"You okay?" he asked.

"I'm fine," I said in a real weak voice. "I'm used to it."

He handed Celie our tickets and said, "The next time, make sure your sister sits with you until the tickets are collected. Not everyone's as easy as I am."

I gave Samantha a big squeeze and another biscuit.

"I'm starved," Celie said. "Let's eat."

She took out the sandwiches and gave me one. Celie's mother was the best sandwich maker. It was fat with cheese and bologna and had lots of mayonnaise. It was so good, but it made me feel kind of sad. I missed my mother's sandwiches. I thought I'd never miss the kind she made, especially the raisin and carrot ones. I gave Samantha some of the cheese. When we finished eating, we were so full we decided to save the fruit for the trip home.

The train made so many stops, it seemed to take longer to get to North Station than Robbie had said it would. When the conductor finally called, "North Station, next, North Station, next!" Celie and I tucked Samantha's head back into the duffel bag and covered her. I held the bag close to me and we started toward the door.

The conductor was standing outside, and when he saw us he said, "Where's your sister?"

Celie pointed to a lady who looked like she could be her mother. "There she is." Then she turned to me and said, "Hurry up, or we'll lose her."

We walked across the street to where the trolleys were and ran for one that said "Park Street." When we got to the Park Street station, Celie went to the information booth. I waited with Samantha. People ran around us, yelling at the trolleys to wait for them. A hundred people passed, but nobody noticed us.

"Come on, Amy," Celie called. "We've got to hurry . . . the trolley to the hospital is coming now." We ran, then climbed aboard and stood as the trolley bounced along. When we heard the conductor call, "Longwood Avenue — Hospital Row," we pushed our way through the crowd and started in the direction of the hospital.

"What if we can't get in?" I said.

"Robbie said he told you how to get in the back way. Don't worry. It'll be all right."

The hospital was a big, ugly, gray stone building, but the stairs Robbie had told me about were beautiful. They looked like the stairs where Cinderella had lost her slipper. But they didn't lead anywhere. Just two sets of stairs that met on a porch with no door to go in. Or out.

"Come on, Amy," Celie said.

We walked around the hospital, and when I saw the "Deliveries Only" sign on the back door, I made sure Samantha was way down in the bag.

Celie opened the door just a little and looked inside. "It's okay," she said. "There's no one around."

We started up the stairs on our tiptoes, and when we got up to the second floor, we waited, listening for footsteps. "All clear," Celie whispered.

We started up to the next floor, but when we got to the landing, we could hear someone coming down. We stood still, not breathing. As the steps got louder and louder, I could feel my heart pounding in my ears. Celie poked my arm and I squeezed Samantha so tight, she started to bark. The footsteps stopped. I whispered to her to please be quiet. Then a door opened and closed and it was still again.

We started up to Robbie's floor, and when we got to the top step, Celie took Samantha while I looked up and down the hallway. There was a light with a sign that said "Nurses' Station." Someone was sitting behind the desk, and a man was walking down the hall, away from where I stood. A red light flashed across the hall and an elevator opened. I saw a boy sitting in a wheelchair with a nurse behind him. She started out. I held my breath and crossed my fingers. "Oops, wrong floor," she said, and backed into the elevator.

I looked around one more time, then took Samantha from Celie's arms. "I'll wait here," Celie said. "I can keep watch." I took a deep breath and walked down the hall until I got to 3H, Robbie's room. He was sleeping.

I looked around the room and saw my mother's sweater on the back of a big chair and some of Robbie's comic books on the end of his bed. But that was all that was any part of home. Everything else was strange. Even the vase filled with flowers on the windowsill.

I walked over to Robbie. He looked so different. His hair was all messy and he was thin and he looked almost as white as the pillow. He never looked like that before. It was almost the end of summer and he didn't even have a tan.

"Robbie," I whispered, "Robbie, it's Amy."

He opened his eyes and smiled the way he always did.

"Hey, Amy, you made it," he said. "I was beginning to think you'd never get here."

As soon as Samantha heard his voice, she began to wiggle in the duffel bag. "Please, don't bark. Please. I'll let you out. Just wait. . . ."

I opened the duffel bag, and she jumped out and fell on the floor. She ran all over the place, she was so happy to see him. Then she slid toward the bed and looked so funny, Rob began to laugh so hard he had to put his face into the pillow.

"Come on, boy," Robbie whispered. "Come on, boy. Come to Robbie."

Samantha leaped from the floor up to Robbie's bed

and licked his face. He wrestled with her for a little bit and then he sank back on the pillow. He looked so tired.

"Thanks for calling Celie," I said. "We made up."

"That's okay," he said. "You shouldn't fight with her. She's your best friend."

"Next to you, Robbie. Next to you."

Samantha kept licking Robbie's face, and he put his arm around her and rubbed her back. "Thanks for bringing him in, Ame. It was great. Look how fat he's getting, and his hair's getting curly. He's just perfect. Isn't he, Amy?"

Robbie's arm was a white stick across Sam's black coat.

"Yeah, Robbie," I said. "He's just perfect."

Robbie looked over at me, and for one little minute his face looked like it used to. "Hey, Amy," he said, "you feeling all right? You actually called Sam a him."

But I couldn't answer him because my nose burned and my eyes stung.

After a while, I said, "You'll never believe it, Rob, there must be a thousand fish in your tank. You're going to have to spend your whole allowance on fish food when you come home."

But Robbie didn't seem interested. He just held Sam in his arms and kept rubbing his fur. "Good old Sam. Good old boy."

He rubbed Sam's belly once more and then put his face in Sam's fur and kissed him. "You be good now. You pay attention to Amy. She's boss for now. You hear me?"

I sat on Robbie's bed and put my hand on his foot. I just wanted to touch him.

Then Robbie put his head back on the pillow and said, "You guys better get home. It's getting late."

I looked at him for a long minute and then I picked Sam up and held him close. I bit my lip so I wouldn't cry. "Say 'So long' to Robbie, Sam. Say 'See you soon, you old pest.' "

Then I took Sam's paw and waved it to Robbie.

Robbie smiled at me and waved his hand. "Thanks, Amy. Thanks a lot. It was good."

I leaned over to kiss him, but then I remembered how he hated that. So I said, "See you, Rob."

"See you, Ame," he said.

I started to open the door. "Amy," Robbie called. "Hey, Amy. Will you do me one more favor?"

"Sure," I said. "Anything."

"Will you paint Sam's doghouse? The summer will be over and he won't even have gotten to cool off in it. It'll be getting cold soon. Paint it yellow like you wanted to. Okay?"

I nodded my head, waved good-bye, and walked to where Celie was waiting. I put my face into Sam's fur, hugged him real hard, and said, "I always knew you were Robbie's dog. I really did."

Then the three of us walked down the stairs and back out the delivery entrance. I turned back once. Just once. And then started home.

"What did Robbie say?" Celie asked.

I shook my head and shrugged my shoulders.

"Did he say when he was coming home?"

I didn't answer her. I held Sam under my arm and walked past the stairs to nowhere and down the street to where the trolley stopped. Celie didn't say anything after that. She took my arm, and the two of us kept walking.

"Do you mind if I sit next to the window?" I asked Celie when we got to North Station.

She shook her head, and I sat at the window seat with Sam on my lap. I didn't put him in the duffel bag; I just covered him with the afghan and rubbed his fur. I felt lonesome. Really lonesome, even with Sam on my lap and Celie beside me.

Another conductor took our tickets and said something about sitting with an adult, but I didn't listen. Celie must have convinced him her sister was somewhere on the train, because he punched our tickets and went on to the next car.

I looked out the window, and even though I could hear the train whistle blow and the sound of the wheels on the tracks, everything seemed so still. It was like the day Baron went to the farm. Only sadder. I put my face against the glass. It felt cool. I closed my eyes and when I did, I saw the vase filled with flowers sitting on Robbie's windowsill. I could even smell them.

"Manuet, next stop," the conductor called out. "Manuet next."

Celie reached over and tapped my arm. "Amy, we're home."

I sat there, not wanting to get off the train, but knowing I had to. I held Sam real tight. We got off the train and walked slowly through town and toward the 88's. We began to climb, and when we got halfway up, I sat down and looked out across the harbor. It was beginning to get dark. Celie sat beside me and said, "We never ate the fruit. Do you want some?"

I shook my head. I just stared out at the lights coming from Boston, thinking about Robbie. Thinking about the day I beat him running up the stairs. I began to shiver even though the stairs were warm under my legs. And then my eyes began to sting real bad. Celie was quiet and Sam was, too.

After a while, we started to climb the stairs one at a time, and when we got to the very top of the 88's, I turned to Celie and said, "I'm getting too old for Mrs. Breene's stories. I don't want to hear them any-more. Especially the one about the graveyard and the kids with their arms sticking up. That's crazy. Isn't it, Celie? Well, isn't it?"

Celie nodded her head. "Sure it is, Amy. It's crazy. Really crazy."

17

"Your mother and father are on their way home," Mrs. Breene called, flashing the porch light on and off. "You'd better start putting all that stuff away."

Celie and I had been working on Sam's house every day since we'd seen Robbie, and tonight we were going to paint it. I moaned and begged Mrs. Breene for a little more time. But she wouldn't listen.

"It's almost ten o'clock, Amy. No more tonight."

I started to pick up the tools and Celie was hammering the paint can cover closed when we heard someone walking through the field.

"Who's there?" I shouted.

"It's me," Jemma said, as she came through the clearing and into the yard. "Celie, Ma says you have to come home."

"But I'm staying with Amy tonight. Pa said I could."

"Celie," Jemma said in a real low voice, "Ma says you have to come home."

The screen door squeaked open, and Mrs. Breene said, "Amy, time to get ready for bed. You come get your things tomorrow, Celie. How's that?"

"That's fine," Jemma said. Then she took Celie's arm and they disappeared into the darkness.

Mrs. Breene told me to be quiet when I started to say how unfair it was for Mrs. DiCarlo to change her mind. "Jemma thinks she's so great, coming over here and pulling Celie home."

She shook her head and locked the screen door. "Go up and get ready for bed," she said. "Your parents will be here by eleven, and Susan's been wanting to talk to you. I'll be up in a few minutes."

My mother had come home twice since Robbie had been in the hospital, and both times she left before I woke up. "Robbie likes me to be there when he wakes up," she'd said when I'd asked her to make muffins for breakfast.

I went up to my room, pulled my bathrobe over my clothes, and went down to Susan's room. The house was cold. It felt more like November than the beginning of September. "Momma's coming home, Susan," I said. "Maybe she'll be here for the first day of school."

Susan was in bed, curled up so that all I could see were her shoulders and a little bit of her hair.

"I think Momma's coming home for good," she said, and her shoulders began to shake, but no sound came.

I pulled my bathrobe around me and crawled into bed beside her. The house was still. I could hear the kitchen floor creak, and then I heard the swoosh of Mrs. Breene's stockings as she came up the stairs and into the room. She sat on the edge of the bed and sighed.

I stared straight up at the ceiling, trying to find the

beginning of the swirls on Susan's ceiling, but I couldn't even find the center. Susan's shoulders shook harder and the bed shivered. A cricket called from the window, and in the distance, I could hear the train whistle blow. I put my hand out and touched Susan. She reached back and took my hand and squeezed it. "Please, God," I whispered, "please, let everything be all right."

After a long while, the lights from my father's car came into the window and I could hear pebbles crunching on the driveway. When the crunching stopped, I heard my father's voice. "Ellen," he said, "we're home."

Susan got out of bed and started downstairs. I heard Mrs. Breene follow her. I didn't want to go. I wanted to go to sleep. I wanted to sleep forever. But after a while, I got up and started down.

"It's not fair," I could hear Susan say. "It's not fair."

I pushed the kitchen door open and saw my father standing next to the stove with Susan. She was sobbing and she kept saying, "It's not fair."

"Life's not fair," my father said in a loud whisper. "Life's not fair."

Then he pulled her to him and hugged her, and when he saw me, he reached out and gathered me in. "He's gone, Amy," he said. "Robbie's gone. God damn it. He didn't make it."

I put my arms around Susan and my father and pressed my face into his shirt. It smelled of sweat and perfume and Robbie's room at the hospital. Susan kept crying and my father held both of us, saying over and over again, "That's it. Cry it all out. Cry it all out."

But I couldn't cry, and after a while, I said, "Where's Momma?"

He motioned toward the living room. I dropped my arms and walked slowly to the door. My legs felt funny, like they were full of pins and needles. The living room was dark, with only a stream of light shining in from the hall, but I could see my mother. She was sitting on the end of the sofa, her back straight, her hands in her lap.

I sat beside her and took her hand. She took a deep breath and started to say something, but her voice wouldn't come.

I put her arm around me and said, "Momma, it's me. Amy. I'm here, Momma."

She nodded and took my hand. And then, as if her voice came through a tunnel, first soft and then louder and louder and louder, she screamed: "Robbie! Robbie! Robbie!"

I pulled away from her and ran out of the living room and through the kitchen. I punched the screen door open and flew into the yard. It was dark, and Sam came after me, whining like he does when he wants to be petted. "Shut up," I screamed. "I hate you. Shut up."

My leg banged against something and I lifted my foot and kicked it. It was the doghouse. "I hate you, too," I screamed. "I hate everybody."

I kicked it until my foot ached. I threw myself on top of the house and pounded it with my fists. Then I picked up the hammer and banged it against the roof, saying, "Why did you do it? You said you'd come home. You promised. You said it. You told me. You told me."

The porch light lit up the backyard, and my father came and took the hammer from my hand. He picked me up and rubbed his face into my hair and said over and over, "It's going to better one day. One day, it's going to be better."

I tried to pull away from him, but he held me tight, and after a while I put my head on his shoulder and closed my eyes.

18

The sound of thunder woke me before I wanted to wake up. Susan was still sleeping beside me, her breath soft and even. I wanted to close my eyes and sleep and sleep and sleep, but I knew I couldn't. The rain beat on the windows and I heard voices coming from down the hall. Dishes rattled in the kitchen, and I could smell coffee. I slipped out of bed and went down to the bathroom with Sam behind me.

Aunt Emma was coming out of the bathroom and Uncle Sam was going in. "You got to use the toilet, Amy?" Uncle Sam asked. "Better do it before I get in there. Takes me a heap of time to shave these days."

I nodded my head, and when I was finished, I thanked him and started down to my room. Aunt Emma and Uncle Sam had come right after my father had told them about Rob, even though Uncle Sam's back was in a big stiff brace. I was glad they were sleeping in my room because I got to sleep with Susan. Nobody even asked to sleep in Rob's room. It was just there, empty and quiet. So quiet I could hear my ears hum whenever I went in. I passed his door and then re- membered I hadn't fed the fish. I went in and sprinkled some food in the tank and watched as they swam up and ate.

The rain came down harder and blew the curtains into the room. A streak of lightning and a crash of thunder came together. The sound of the rain made me feel so lonesome. "Looks like we're in for a bad storm this mornin'," I could hear Uncle Sam say as he passed Rob's room. And this morning we were going to the funeral home to bring Robbie's clothes. Mr. Devine, the funeral man, told my mother he thought Robbie should wear a suit and a tie. "Most folks like formality," he'd told my mother.

"But I don't," she'd said. And then she'd told him we'd bring him what Robbie was to wear.

I swished the water around in the tank and then went over to Robbie's closet. I stood there for a long time thinking about what he'd want to wear. My mother had told Susan and me we could pick out whatever we thought he'd like. Susan said she couldn't do it, but I wanted to. I took his red sweater from the shelf, the one he always wore because he said it didn't itch him. Then I took down his best pair of corduroy pants, the pair he wore when he wanted to impress Gloreen. I got matching socks and I even shined his shoes. Then I spread everything out on the bed and called my mother.

She stood and looked at them for a long time, and after a while, she picked up his red sweater and held it up to her face. The sleeves lay flat against her skirt. Then she put Rob's pants over her arm and asked me to bring his shoes and socks. "Don't forget some underwear, Amy." Then she closed Robbie's closet door very slowly and stood there. I looked at her, and in my whole life, I never saw her look the way she did then. Standing in the middle of Robbie's room with the sleeve of his sweater hanging down on her foot, she looked beautiful. Even though she looked tired and sad and her eyes were red and watery, she looked beautiful. And she looked strong. She looked so strong, it made me feel safe.

"These are just fine," Mr. Devine said in a kindly voice when we gave him Robbie's clothes. And then he went over to my father and said, "He'll be ready by one o'clock. Most folks like to come by early, before calling hours begin."

My father nodded and told Mr. Devine we'd go home for some lunch and come back at one. "I appreciate your kindness," my father said.

Mrs. Breene made grilled cheese sandwiches. But nobody ate much. Susan squeezed the cheese out of the sides and licked it off. I didn't even take one bite of mine.

Then we put on our church clothes and it was time to go.

My father took my mother's arm when we got to the funeral home and the two of them went up to see Rob. My father's whole body began to sob, and my mother kept rubbing his back over and over again. After a long time, she bent down and kissed Robbie and then she motioned for Susan and me to come over.

I didn't want to go, but Susan went and looked down at Robbie. Her shoulders began to shake.

I felt a big lump starting in my throat and I wanted to cry, but I didn't let myself because I knew if I did, I might never stop. Then my mother would start to cry and my father would cry more and I couldn't stand that.

I walked over to Robbie, my nails digging into my hands. He was so still. His face looked like wax and somebody had combed his hair flat down. His hands were crossed, and when I touched them, they were cold and hard. I tried to pull his fingers apart, but they didn't move. I looked at him for a long time, trying to find him, but all that was really him were his clothes.

Gloreen came to see Robbie and so did Bootsy. Celie stayed with me and told me she would be at the church service with her mother and Jemma later on. Miss Finnegan came with some other teachers and lots of kids from the junior high. Robbie's whole class came. Even Miss Swords came.

After everybody left the funeral home and it was time to take Robbie to church, the whole family went up to say good-bye to him. Mr. Devine motioned for me to come up, but I shook my head and stood alone at the back of the room. I didn't want to see Robbie like that again. Everything about him different, every part of him cold and still.

Everybody said the service was wonderful, the flowers were beautiful, the casket just lovely, and all those dumb things. The priest came to the cemetery, even though it was a long ride. He said some prayers, and when he was finished, he shook hands with my father and kissed my mother. Then Mr. Devine said it was time to go.

The ride home was a long one and everybody tried to make some talk about how nice Miss Swords looked, how terrible Mr. Burns looked, and how nice it was of Celie and her mother and Jemma to come to the service. And how good it was of everybody to understand that just the family was to go to the cemetery. "Wasn't it nice of Mrs. DiCarlo to bake all those lovely cookies?" Aunt Emma said. But nobody answered her.

The rain looked like wrinkled sheets of cellophane on the car windows, and the windshield wipers thumped back and forth. Mr. Devine tried to joke about how he wouldn't have to wash his limousine for a while. "Stupid old man," I said under my breath.

"What's that you said, Amy?" Uncle Sam asked.

And then we were home.

19

I hated to go back to school. It wasn't because I was up in the sixth grade or anything like that. It was just different.

Everybody tried to be so nice. "What a pleasure it is to have you in my class," Miss Alexander said. "We'll have a really good year."

Roberta tried to be nice, but I wouldn't let her. Peter asked me to play stickball with him one day, but I didn't. He told me he was really sorry he'd been so mean. He even said Roberta was sorry, but I didn't believe him. Only Celie was the same. Only Celie tried to talk about Robbie, but I always stopped her. Nobody else mentioned him. Except once.

"Amy, would you step into the cloakroom?" Miss Alexander asked me one Friday in late September.

Nobody ever went into the cloakroom with the teacher unless they'd done something terrible, and I hadn't done anything at all.

Miss Alexander always dressed in dark blue. She was very tall and wore glasses with wire rims. Her nose was very big. "Amy," she said in a soft voice, "how are you doing? Would you like to tell me about Robbie?"

I shook my head. She put her hand on my shoulder. I looked up and kept my eyes on her nostrils, trying to count the little hairs that I saw. I bit my lip and said nothing. I prayed I wouldn't cry, because all the kids were in the classroom, waiting for the three o'clock bell to ring.

She smiled at me and wished me a good weekend and then she said, "Amy, you're a brave girl."

I thanked her and walked out of the cloakroom. The bell rang, and Celie and I started for home. Celie asked if everything was all right. "Yes," I said. And then we were silent.

I hated weekends, too. Especially Sundays. Everybody tried to be busy and extra polite to everybody else. Aunt Emma and Uncle Sam had come every Sunday since Robbie died, and the Sunday that Susan was sixteen, my mother invited Stanley. She asked Mr. and Mrs. Breene, too, but Mr. Breene didn't want to come. My mother made Susan's favorite dinner, and when it was time for Susan to blow out the candles on her cake, Aunt Emma reminded her to make a wish. Sue said she was too old for that and blew them out. She missed two candles.

Everybody began to talk about everything, even about Robbie. Everybody but me.

"Did I tell you how Baron rounds up Elmer and Sari every sundown and gets them into the barn?" Uncle Sam asked me.

"Yes," I said. And to myself, I said, "About a million times."

After dinner, I went outside. The sun was almost

gone, and it was cool. I got on the swing and looked around the yard. My father's shirts were hanging on the clothesline, with my mother's slips and Susan's blouse. And my plaid dress. It made me think about the night Mrs. Van had locked me out and how I'd shone the flashlight all around the house. First the kitchen. Then the dining room. Then Robbie's room. I remembered how the leaves from the willow tree had made designs on Robbie's window.

Tonight the house was a big paper cutout against the sky, and as the lights came on inside the house, I could see my mother standing at the kitchen window, my father beside her. Mrs. Breene and Aunt Emma sat at the dining room table, talking. Uncle Sam must have been in the downstairs bathroom, because the light came on in there. I looked up at Robbie's window, pretending he was somewhere in his room, waiting for me. But it was black, and in the stillness I could hear the willow branches scratch against the glass.

I pulled Sam toward me, and for the first time since Robbie died, I started to cry. I didn't want to. I didn't want to have to cry, because somewhere inside me I knew when I cried, Robbie would really be gone and I'd never see him again.

My mouth was dry, and the taste of salt was on my lips. I wiped my face on my sleeve and whispered, "I wrecked it, Rob. I wrecked the doghouse. Did you hear me? I wrecked the doghouse."

And then I began to sob softly into the quiet, cool air.

"Amy," I heard my father's voice call. He came and

stood over me. He held the sides of the swing and began to push it. After a while, he sat down beside me and handed me some tissues. "I've got more in my pocket," he said, putting his arm around my shoulder.

"Thanks," I said, blowing my nose with one and drying my face with another.

He pushed the swing for a long time, not saying anything, and then he took in a big breath and breathed out a big sigh. "Amy," he said, "today is Sunday and it happens to be Sue's birthday. Tomorrow is Monday, and in a little while, Thanksgiving and Christmas will come. And then spring. Then summer. And before you know it, it will be Sue's birthday again."

I blew my nose and looked toward the field.

He pulled me closer.

"I miss him," I said.

"I know."

"I'll never stop missing him."

"Do you think I'll ever stop missing him? Or your mother? Or Sue? Some days I pretend it hasn't happened."

"Do you think he misses me?"

My father nodded.

"If I could just see him again," I said.

My father hugged me to him, and we rocked, his feet pushing the swing back and forth, his woolen jacket scratching my cheek.

"Maybe it's like Baron out at the farm," I said, trying so hard to believe that some part of Robbie would never leave me. "We couldn't see him every day, but we knew he was there and he was happy."

"That's right," he whispered. "That's right."

We rocked for a long time; the light in Susan's room went on, and music drifted from the window. Sam wiggled out of my lap and ran around the swing. And in the distance, a train whistle blew.

"You ready to go in?" my father asked.

I shook my head.

We rocked for a while, and when the swing slowed down, he said, "I think I'll go in to see if I can help your mother." Then he took his jacket off and put it around me. "Amy," he said, kissing my forehead, "I like you. Come inside before it gets too dark."

He started toward the house, Sam at his heels, and then turned and said, "How about if I get Sam's house ready for painting?"

I didn't answer him.

I waited until I heard the porch door close behind him. Then I got up and walked over to the house. It was like a tiny chapel, sitting all alone. Still and quiet, nothing moving around it.

I pulled my father's jacket around me and walked past the house, and down the path and onto the sidewalk. I passed Miss Swords's house, dark as always. I passed the road leading to the field that joined Celie's yard to mine. I walked past the convent yard. I walked until I was where I needed to go. To the top of the 88's. I sat down. The stairs were rough and damp under my legs, and I shivered, but I didn't feel cold.

I sat there for a long time wishing and wishing, but knowing those wishes couldn't come true, knowing things would never really be the same again. After a while I walked down the stairs, one by one, and when I got to the bottom, I got a strange, kind of weird, feeling. It was like Robbie was there. I really felt like he was there, only I couldn't see him. I stood still, barely breathing. I didn't feel scared or anything. Just different. Better, almost.

When the street lamps came on, I remembered my father had told me to be home before dark, so I started back up the stairs, slowly. I thought about Sam's house and how Rob had told me I could paint it yellow, like I'd wanted to. I started to cry again. But I didn't try to stop. I kept crying until I couldn't cry anymore. Then I wiped my face, looked over my shoulder, and whispered, "Race you up the stairs."

I took them two at a time, running as fast as I could, and when I got to the top, I said, "Okay. Okay. You beat me. You win."

And then I kept running. Past the convent yard. Past the road leading to Celie's yard and mine. Past Miss Swords's house. I raced down the street toward our house, and when I saw the light shining on our porch and heard my father calling to me, I flew up the stairs and threw myself at him. I hugged him hard and said, "If you fix Sam's house, Dad, I'll paint it yellow, just like Rob said. But the roof will be blue. Bright blue. A nice, bright sunny sky blue."